A SUSPICIOUS
PROPOSAL

A SUSPICIOUS PROPOSAL

BY

HELEN BROOKS

MILLS & BOON®

First published in Great Britain 2000
Large Print edition 2000
Harlequin Mills & Boon Limited,
Eton House, 18-24 Paradise Road,
Richmond, Surrey TW9 1SR

© Helen Brooks 2000

ISBN 0 263 16717 8

Set in Times Roman 16½ on 17½ pt.
16-1100-56260

Printed and bound in Great Britain
by Antony Rowe Ltd, Chippenham, Wiltshire

CHAPTER ONE

OH, SHE felt dodgy, she really did. Why, oh, why had she had that crab and prawn cocktail at the hotel last night, when she'd known at the first mouthful it didn't taste quite right? Stupid, stupid, stupid!

'And do you, Christine Harper, take Enoch Charles Brown…?'

Enoch? For a moment, Essie's thoughts lifted from the state of her stomach and swirling head and focused on the couple standing at the altar in front of her. Fancy old Charlie having Enoch for his first name! He'd kept that quiet all through veterinary college—but then she couldn't really blame him. Had Chris known Charlie wasn't really Charlie but an Enoch in disguise?

It was just at that moment that Christine turned her head in its swathe of chiffon edged with sequins and gazed up adoringly into Charlie's handsome face, and Essie reflected wryly that it wouldn't have made any difference if Chris had known or not. Her friend was

head over heels in love with her dashing veterinary surgeon and had been from the very
second their eyes had met on the first morning
of college. And now here they all were, a few
short years later, in Christine's quaint little
parish church in Stafford.

As the vicar's voice droned on, Essie's eyes
wandered from the back of the frothy lace figure in front of her to her own pale lemon satin-
bedecked shape. She wished this was over.
The pills Christine's mother had insisted she
take that morning—'The chief bridesmaid
can't go hopping off to the loo halfway
through the service, now then, Essie. Take
these and you'll get through without any problems'—had seemed to stop the more unpleasant manifestations of the touch of food poisoning she was experiencing, but the fact that she
had been up all night and hadn't dared to eat
a thing that morning was making her feel very
peculiar.

She wished she could slip these precariously
high-heeled shoes off. They were pinching like
mad. Essie surreptitiously tried to ease her aching toes but nearly overbalanced in the pro-
cess, only the quick steadying hand of
Janice—Christine's cousin—at the side of her

preventing her from catapulting into the pair in front.

It was as Essie was giving a weak smile of thanks to the grinning Janice that she noticed him. He was staring, openly, from his vantage point in the pew adjoining the aisle, and he was a big man—but purely in the muscular sense; she doubted if there was an ounce of spare flesh anywhere on the lean, finely honed male frame. His hair was jet-black, almost a blue-black, and his skin was very tanned, emphasising the ice-blue of the narrowed eyes still more.

And it was the eyes that caused Essie's face to straighten with an abruptness born of shock. They were disapproving. No, more than that, she corrected herself silently; they were positively *scathing*.

She tore her mesmerised gaze away, jerking her head to the front again as she forced herself to take a long deep breath and count to ten, but she couldn't do anything about the tell-tale colour flooding her skin.

How dared he look at her like that? she asked herself furiously, her cheeks burning. The cold eyes had been withering, his mouth quite literally curling at the edges with a scorn that was searing. And she had never seen him before in her life. She knew she hadn't. Him, she would have remembered!

Her agitation wasn't helping either her stomach or her fuzzy head and Essie tried desperately to concentrate on nothing but the scene being enacted in front of her; then, as the minister indicated for the bride and groom and their respective parents—along with the best man—to follow him out into the little vestry at the rear of the church, she was able to move forward and sink down onto the front pew and ease her shaking legs, blessing the fact that the tiny room had been considered too small to take the bridesmaids.

Who was he? Under cover of a very plump lady singing a solo spirited rendition of 'Love Found a Way' at a volume that made the eyeballs rattle, Essie whispered the thought to Janice. 'Don't look now, Jan, but there's a man in the second pew from the front, a...tall man. Do you know who he is?'

'You mean Xavier Grey.' Janice didn't even have to think about it and there was definite relish in her voice when she said, 'He's gorgeous, isn't he? Not exactly handsome in the traditional sense—but he's got something that makes the toes curl, all right.'

'Gorgeous' was not the adjective Essie would have chosen and her tone reflected this when she said, 'You know him, then?'

'I know *of* him.' There was a definite note of wistful longing in Janice's voice. 'Apparently he's Charlie's—or should I say Enoch's—' Janice dug Essie in the ribs with a wicked chuckle '—second cousin twice removed or some such thing. Aunt June—' Christine's mother '—said there was some sort of family quarrel years ago, from what she can make out, and the feud's continued right up until this wedding brought some sort of reconciliation.'

'Oh, right.' Essie nodded her blonde head and then bent a little closer as the warbling refrains of 'Love lifted me from depths of woe to endless day' drowned Janice's next words.

'What?' she whispered enquiringly.

'I said, I notice he's got seated right at the front with the immediate family,' Janice whispered back meaningfully. And then, at Essie's puzzled frown she added cryptically, 'He's stinking rich.'

'Stinking...?'

'Well, it's obvious, isn't it?' Janice murmured softly. 'Charlie's parents want to get in
with him, now everyone's chummy again; a
millionaire in the family isn't to be sneezed at.'

'Is he? A millionaire, I mean?'

'Too true.' Janice sighed longingly, her
rosy-cheeked plain face mournful. 'It's not
fair, is it, that some lucky woman will get all
that—wealth, a life of ease and comfort, and
Xavier Grey to wake up to in the morning.'

'He might be a real pig when you get to
know him,' Essie said flatly.

'With all that he's got going for him, I'd
excuse him anything.' Janice grinned back,
just as the last note of music died away. The
rest of the congregation took a deep reviving
breath and savoured the blissful silence for a
moment, before shuffling to their feet as the
bridal pair emerged from the back of the
church, their faces beaming.

The next hour consisted of endless photographs under the voluptuous blossom of the
cherry trees surrounding the square of village
green and, although Essie felt a little better in
the fresh May air, it was still an effort for her
to smile brightly and act normally when her
stomach kept growling like a bear with a sore

head. But the light spring breeze and soft golden sunshine had cleared her muzzy head by the time the bridesmaids were all back in the second wedding car, being transported to the wedding reception some five miles away.

There were more photographs in the elegant foyer of the luxurious hotel where the wedding lunch was being held—the foyer had its own miniature waterfall, which the photographers enthused over—but then they were all seated on the top table and Essie could kick off her shoes and relax back in her seat.

But only for a second. Then her eyes met the piercingly silver-blue gaze she had been avoiding for the last hour and a half, and she realised in that instant that she had been aware of Xavier Grey every moment of the time that had elapsed since that first shock of eye-contact in the church. He'd been watching her, and the quality of his scrutiny hadn't changed—it was still derisive.

She stared back over the tables into the hard, aggressively masculine face, her deep violet-blue eyes betraying none of the apprehension and unease which was causing her heart to pound like a drum.

What was the matter with him? she asked herself as a waiter moved between them, breaking the eye-contact and allowing her to sink back again, her cheeks flushed and hot. He was acting as though he knew her, as though she had done something awful. Had he mistaken her for someone else? Was that it? It was certainly the only explanation that made any sense.

The meal, in spite of the lavish surroundings, was mediocre, but Essie managed a few mouthfuls of each course—enough not to bring any attention to herself, anyway. She was seated next to the best man, Charlie's brother, who was married with a very pregnant wife he blatantly adored, and for most of the lunch he regaled her with the intricacies of antenatal classes and the baby books he had read, but in such a purposely amusing way that the two of them were convulsed with laughter every few minutes. And she made absolutely sure she didn't glance Xavier Grey's way again. But he was watching her. She just knew it.

The speeches over, the wedding cake cut and the drinks flowing freely was the signal for the radiant bride and groom to take the floor for the first dance, and Essie found herself misty-eyed at the look on Christine's face as she gazed up at her new husband.

She was glad it had worked out for Christine, she thought warmly; she really was. Charlie had had something of a roving eye at veterinary college, and there had been times when Essie had been fearful he was playing fast and loose. But here he was, the devoted bridegroom, and Christine had fulfilled her dearest wish and was now Mrs Brown. A classic happy ending, and you didn't get too many of those these days. She pushed the somewhat cynical thought aside abruptly, cross that she had let it surface on Christine's wedding day, and took a long swallow from her glass of tonic water.

'I'd go careful with that, if I were you.'

The deep, husky and very sexy Canadian drawl brought Essie's head swinging round and then she froze, the smile dying from her face and her thought processes freezing.

Close up, Xavier Grey was even bigger than she had thought—six foot two or three easily—but it was the overall *hardness* of him that had caused her brain to stop. The rugged toughness of the uncompromisingly cold face, the lean, powerful body, the big-muscled

shoulders all spoke of a male strength and
power that was formidable. He looked hard-
bitten and shrewd and unsentimental, and he
scared her to death.

'Careful with…?'

Her echo of his words was spoken uncon-
sciously; all lucid thought was taken up with
the frightening giant in front of her. But then,
as he nodded again towards the glass in her
hand and said, his voice cool and compelling,
'Shouldn't you try and remain *compos mentis*
in case Christine needs you?' she understood
what he was insinuating. 'Champagne is supposed to be sipped, not consumed in great
gulps,' he continued conversationally.

Champagne? He'd assumed her sensible
tonic water was champagne? Essie thought be-
wilderedly, closely followed with, How dared
he anyway? And what was it to do with him
if she drank bottles of champagne?

'Look, I'm sorry but—'

'I understand the hen party was a riot—' the
hateful, easy drawl was patronising '—but
dancing on the table and being carried home
from the pub is one thing, the wedding day is
another. You were clearly toting the mother
and father of a hangover in church; don't you

think you owe it to Christine to conduct your-self properly today?'

She stared at him, too flabbergasted to speak. It had been Janice who had overimbibed at the hen party the night before and had been carried home; but, as Janice herself had said cheerfully that morning, when they were climbing into their bridesmaid's dresses, she had a cast-iron stomach and never woke with a hangover. 'Of course, the parties at college are a good training ground,' the other girl had admitted brightly, 'and my evening job at the Sportsman's Arms helps, too. Still, I'll have to start watching it, I suppose. I did make some-thing of a spectacle of myself last night, didn't I?'

Essie had grinned at the frankly unabashed face in front of her and made some soothing comment—she couldn't remember what, now. Janice was twenty years old, big, heavy, and not even her mother could have called her pretty, but there was a charm about the utterly unpretentious girl that was very endearing. And she *had* been comical the night before—hilarious, in fact. But suddenly it all didn't seem so amusing.

Xavier Grey was smiling at her now, and his tone was definitely condescending when he added, 'I understand you're doing Theatre Studies at college, Janice? You're hoping to go on the stage?' His ice-blue eyes lingered on her mass of silky golden curls that would never be restrained, the huge violet-blue eyes with their thick, thick lashes and the perfect creamy skin.

Essie opened her mouth to tell him of his mistake a second before full realisation hit, turning her eyes dark purple. Xavier had clearly been informed of the antics of the night before by one of his relatives, and when he had seen herself and Janice he had automatically labelled her the giddy college student with the part-time job as a barmaid. And why? Essie stared at the strong-featured, vigorous face in front of her. Because she was the typical male perception of a blonde bimbo, that was why!

All her life she had been dogged by this particular mentality from a certain section of the opposite sex, and it grated—it grated unbearably, and never as much as now. There were some men who even seemed to take it as some sort of personal insult when they found out she was a darn sight more intelligent than them; that she had a brain and knew how to use it. She had got three straight As in her A Levels, and at veterinary college she had more than held her own with her male colleagues, in spite of weighing just nine stone and being five foot seven.

'Go on the stage?' She turned in her seat, the pale lemon satin of her dress and the fresh daisies threaded in the gold of her hair adding to the impression of a young girl barely out of her teens. That was another thing that always proved awkward, especially when she had been doing her veterinary training. It hadn't been so bad at the surgery, with the domestic animals, but when she had gone out to the farms to deal with a poorly heifer or another of the large animals some of the farmers had been totally dumbstruck.

'Or are your sights set even higher? Maybe Hollywood?'

Oh, yes, he *definitely* had her labelled as the hopeful little blonde starlet, Essie told herself savagely: all hair and breasts and cotton wool where her brain should have been. He'd be saying next he knew a Hollywood producer or something, and maybe she'd like to come out to the back seat of his car to discuss it. But no, not the back seat, she silently corrected herself in the next moment—nothing so tacky for Xavier Grey. It would be a full dinner and hotel room for this man.

He needed taking down a peg or two. The thought had been there from the first moment she had seen him but now crystallised into firm conviction. And, if he did but know it, he had given her the perfect opportunity to do just that, because, along with the unmistakable condescension, there was something else staring out of the dark male face and she had seen it in too many other men to doubt it. He fancied her. Physically, he fancied her very much, although it was clear he thought her mind was way, way below his notice.

'Hollywood?' Essie put a coo into her voice that was so hammed up that, for a moment, she thought she had overdone it. But he swallowed it, hook, line and sinker. 'Little old me?' She pouted slightly, allowing her full rosebud mouth to send out an invitation as old as time. 'You're teasing me.'

'Not at all,' he responded gallantly. 'You can do anything you want in life if you're determined enough.'

Oh, she was determined, all right—determined to teach Xavier Grey a lesson he would never forget!

'You really think so?' She let the full sweep of her thick dark lashes cover her eyes for a moment before raising them again to look straight into his face.

'Of course. Look at Christine and Essie,' Xavier said quietly, sliding into the seat Charlie's brother had recently vacated when he had gone to sit with his wife and her parents, once the dancing had started. 'They would have been very much the exception to the rule, even as short a time as a couple of decades ago, but more and more women are becoming veterinary surgeons now. Of course, others are more suited to less...physically demanding careers,' he added softly, his eyes moving over her delicate loveliness again.

'You think Essie looks the part, is that it?' Essie asked with determined innocence, opening her eyes very wide. 'She is quite strong.'

'I'm sure she is.' Xavier glanced across to where Janice was dancing an energetic foxtrot with one of the guests, her thick-set, strapping frame straining the pale lemon satin to excess.

'And perfectly suited for her chosen profession, as you are for yours.'

Oh, you utter, absolute male chauvinist pig, you. Essie had to look down quickly before he saw the blaze of anger in her eyes.

'Would you care to dance?'

He had clearly taken her action as a form of coquetry—she could read it in the slightly amused, resigned note hidden in the deep voice—and now she raised her eyes again, pushing back the soft curls that had fallen about her face as she said brightly, 'That would be lovely, thank you.'

'The pleasure will be all mine.'

The flirting was obvious but circumspect, Essie thought cynically, rising gracefully to her feet after slipping her shoes on. She had to admit that, for all his rugged hardness, he was a smooth devil when he wanted to be.

She was aware of more than one frankly envious pair of female eyes following her as she made her way to the dance floor with Xavier's hand in the small of her back, and wondered what all those women would think if they knew what she was about. But they didn't: and, more importantly, neither did Xavier Grey. Of course, it would only take one person to call her by name for her little ruse to be brought out into the open, but hopefully she could continue it for a little longer. It was going to be so sweet to see the look on his arrogant male face when he realised he'd been taken for a ride.

And few of the guests knew her. She hugged the thought to her as she turned and allowed him to take her into his arms. When she had met Christine at university, the two of them had become immediate best friends, their delight when they were both accepted for the same veterinary college exuberant. But she had only visited Christine's family once or twice in the intervening years, due to the fact that she—unlike Christine—did not have well-to-do parents supporting her. She had needed to work every minute she could at weekends and in the holidays to pay the innumerable expenses involved in the training for the career she loved so passionately. So it might be a while yet before her deception was discovered by the big hard man holding her close.

Too close. She looked up past the massive width of his shoulders and the silver-blue eyes were waiting for her, their expression unfathomable.

Essie smiled, but coolly this time, easing herself from the large, lean frame as she said, 'I'm sorry, I don't think you told me your name?'

There was a momentary flicker of surprise in the narrowed gaze—which Essie counted as a small triumph; he had clearly assumed *everyone* knew who the great Xavier Grey was, she thought nastily—before he said, 'I'm sorry. How remiss of me. I think I must have assumed your aunt and uncle would have told you the names of the new contingent added to Enoch's family.' His tone was wry. 'My name is Xavier Grey and I am totally at your disposal.'

Far more than he thought, right at this moment. Essie smiled sweetly.

'Hello, Xavier Grey,' she said with honeyed charm.

'Hello, Janice.' He was out to seduce, all right. The deep voice was seriously sensual, and Essie could have giggled if it weren't for the sudden alarms that had gone off all over her body. He was too good at this, that was the trouble, she told herself quickly, and in this particular instance that suggested a great deal of experience. The warm, smoky tone of his

voice, the mellowing of that harsh, rugged face
and the deliciously tempting smell of his af-
tershave all spoke of a dedicated wolf in
sheep's clothing. Well, perhaps not his after-
shave, she admitted to herself in the next instant; that was probably just part of the man
himself. But the rest... It was a definite practised, tried and tested come-on and no doubt
had rendered Xavier dividends in the past. But
not today, and not with her.

She nestled back against him, trying to ignore how perfectly her head fitted under his
chin and how it felt to be in the arms of a
virile, powerful man like him, telling herself
she owed it to all the other women in the world
to teach him that all cats weren't grey in the
dark. But the touch of sanctimonious self-
righteousness was swiftly dispelled by her innate honesty. She was doing this for herself,
no one else and he deserved it; he really did.

'How old are you, Janice?'

There was a note to his voice now she
couldn't quite place and it made her tilt her
face to his again. 'You mean the family grape-
vine hasn't dotted the i's and crossed the t's?'
she asked lightly. 'I would have thought you'd

have been given the low-down, on both sides, to the last tiny detail.'

His eyes crinkled and her stomach flipped, and this time it was nothing to do with the crab and prawn cocktail. 'Family gossip is the worst thing,' he agreed softly.

'Isn't it just?' She dimpled up at him, batting her eyelashes in true Hollywood style. 'But thorough.'

'You're twenty years old, unattached, and determined to branch out into the precarious world of entertainment—their opinion, not mine,' he added hastily.

'That's what they told you about little old Janice Beaver?' Essie asked teasingly.

'Uh-huh.'

'Then I guess I can't argue with it.'

He nodded slowly. 'How old do you think I am?' he asked after a long moment.

Oh, help. Essie kept her face fixed in its come-hither mode as her mind sought a throwaway line to finish what had become a minefield and came up empty. 'I don't know; thirty, thirty-one maybe?' she suggested with a winsome smile. He looked to be in his late thirties, maybe early forties, but that wouldn't win her any prizes in this sweepstake.

'You're being kind.' He grinned down at her and again her body responded with frightening immediacy to the lethal male charm that was becoming stronger every second she was with him. 'I'm thirty-three,' he said softly, 'but I know I look a good few years older.'

She couldn't think of a thing to say, so she batted her eyelashes again for good measure and shrugged offhandedly. 'I'm not into this age thing.' She wrinkled her small nose at him provocatively. 'Toy-boys, toy-girls, sugar-daddies and all that—so what? It's just society putting labels on people when all's said and done, don't you think?' And then, as the some-what sombre waltz changed to a pop number and disco lights began to flash, she added, 'Prepare your ears for blasting. Christine gave in to the first three dances being formal but the rest of the music is her and Charlie's choice and they're into soul and rock and roll.'

'Great. Time for a drink, I think.' As the hard male body straightened away from her, she was shocked at the sudden sense of loss she felt, but then he was guiding her towards the bar and, to her horror, she saw Charlie's brother and his wife and in-laws in a little

group directly in front of them. It was too soon
to blow her cover!

'I'll wait here.' She ducked into a small al-
cove, but not before he had followed her eyes.

'Right.' The warmth had gone from his
voice and now his eyes were blue ice. 'Went
a bit too far, did you?'

'I beg your pardon?' She stared at him, utterly at a loss.

'With Edward.' He indicated Charlie's
brother with a wave of his hand. 'I noticed you
two were getting on rather well during the
meal. Wife objected, did she?'

'What?' She didn't believe this man; she really didn't. First he had her typecast as a fluffy
little coquette without a brain in her head and
now she was a would-be husband-stealer, too!
The man was obsessed. She knew she'd gone
scarlet—temper always affected her that
way—but just as she opened her mouth to tell
him exactly what she thought of him a portly
matron—a vision in bright pink and mauve—
descended on them. Her red-painted mouth
was already gushing how absolutely wonderful
it was to see him, she'd heard *so* much about
him, and hadn't it been a positively *divine* service?

Xavier was polite, just about, but his voice was cool with a satirical bite and the woman didn't linger. Nevertheless, it gave Essie a few precious moments to gather her wits and take control of her tongue. He'd pay for that last remark. Not yet, no—she'd take this as far as it could go—but it would make the moment he found out he'd been made a prize fool of all the more precious. What gave him the right to set himself up as judge and jury on other people, anyway? she thought tightly as she watched him make his way to the bar after he had asked her what she would like to drink. She had thought of asking for a double brandy or something similar—to fit the image—but, just in case he took her at her word, she hadn't dared. Her delicate stomach couldn't cope with anything stronger than tonic water.

By the time he returned, Essie was fully into the part she was playing again. As they sat down at a vacant table, she set to with gusto, regaling him with a few of the anecdotes Janice had told them last night about her life at college—and out of it—especially the more outrageous bits. Janice had had no compunction in revealing she was no vestal virgin, and now, as Essie related the other girl's stories, she had the added advantage of authenticity.

And yet she wasn't getting quite the reaction she had expected, she admitted to herself after some time had passed. He ought to be congratulating himself that he was on to a good thing, but if he was he was hiding it well, she thought caustically. The air of disapproval was stronger now, if anything.

'You'll burn yourself out if you're not careful.' His voice was abrupt after she had giggled her way through Janice's antics at the college Christmas party, which were definitely X-rated.

Funnily enough, it was exactly what she herself had said to Janice the night before, and now she gave the answer Janice had given her in the same flippant tone the other girl had used. 'Life's for living and I want to get the most I can out of mine.'

'I think you've made that very clear,' he said grimly.

'And you?' She leant forward now, just close enough so her perfume—a wildly expensive one that Christine and Charlie had given her and Janice to thank them for being bridesmaids—tickled his senses and the soft silk of her hair brushed his face for a moment. 'What about you?' she asked softly. 'Don't you believe in having a good time?'

'Oh, yes, Janice. I believe in having a good time,' he said with a sudden silky dangerousness that caused the alarm bells to start ringing.

She was out of her league here. A tiny voice in Essie's head shouted the warning. She had been playing with fire, and, if she wasn't very careful, she might well get burnt. A little shiver of something hot—fear, excitement, desire? She wasn't sure—flickered down her spine, igniting something deep in the core of her.

'There you are, then,' she said huskily, and the throatiness wasn't at all feigned. Janice had been right when she'd said Xavier Grey had something, and that something was lethal. Call it sheer old-fashioned sex appeal or animal magnetism or whatever—he had it all right. And he knew how to use it when he wanted to, Essie thought weakly. One minute the cool, aloof ice-man, the next a seductive, fascinating charmer with more pulling power than a hundred icons of the silver screen.

'Look, I'm going to have to circulate for a while.' She stood up abruptly and she wouldn't

admit to herself it was due to panic. 'We've
been talking for nearly an hour and as—' she
nearly said 'chief bridesmaid' and checked
herself just in time, in case he'd been told that
job was Essie's '—a bridesmaid there are certain duties expected of me.'

'Of course.' He had risen to his feet with
her and now he nodded, his manner easy. 'Just
one thing…'

'Yes?' He had paused and now Essie looked
up at him enquiringly. 'What is it?'

'Come back to me.' His voice was deep and
low and the heat inside her burnt stronger.
Which was ridiculous, just plain ridiculous,
she told herself feverishly, hearing her voice
make some light reply even as her mind
worked quite separately. He was an experi-
enced man of the world, a powerful, rich bach-
elor who was used to women lining up for him,
and an encounter like this would mean nothing
to him.

And what was this encounter, anyway? she
asked herself with a touch of hidden hysteria
as she walked across the room to where Janice
was sitting—with characteristic abandon-
ment—with her shoes off and her feet resting

on another chair. It was a fabrication, an illusion.

'I see you've made a conquest.' Janice's voice was utterly without malice as she glanced up at the slim, beautiful girl in front of her. 'He hasn't taken his eyes off you all day.'

'No.' Essie looked down at the other girl and came to an instant decision, plumping down beside her and leaning forward conspiratorially. 'Actually, Jan, it isn't as straightforward as it looks.'

'What isn't?'

'Me and Xavier Grey. He thinks I'm you,' Essie said quietly.

'What?' Janice jerked her feet to the floor. 'How on earth did he come to think that?' she asked in bewilderment. 'And why haven't you told him who you really are?'

'Well, it was like this...' As Essie began to explain, Janice's eyes began to twinkle, and by the time she had finished, the other girl was giggling unrestrainedly.

'Serves him right.' She glanced across the room and then back to Essie. 'And it's pretty insulting to me, too, if you think about it. I might not be God's gift to the male sex, but I can still get the odd fella's juices going, I can tell you.'

'I don't doubt it for a minute.' Essie grinned back, and then, as their gazes met and held, both girls collapsed into helpless laughter.

'So when are you going to tell him?' Janice asked, once they had composed themselves.

'I don't know.' Essie shrugged her slim shoulders. 'When I'm tumbled, I suppose; someone is bound to drop me in it eventually.'

'Talking of tumbling...' Janice's face was suddenly serious as she looked into the deep violet-blue eyes in front of her. 'He's got a bit of a reputation, Essie, so watch yourself. He's the original cool love-'em-and-leave-'em type; never gets involved and plays strictly by his own rules. According to Aunt June, he has women throwing themselves at him all the time; but as soon as it looks like getting serious it's curtains. He's not a man to mess with.'

'I don't intend to mess with him, Jan, not in that sense, anyway,' Essie said firmly. 'He's arrogant and rude and overbearing—'

'And gorgeous.' Janice's voice was full of laughter now. 'You have to admit that, Essie, even if you don't like him. He's totally drop-dead gorgeous. That mixture of cool control and ruthlessness is dynamite and, when added to his looks and the fact that he's absolutely loaded...what an aphrodisiac!'

'Jan, you're awful.' Essie pushed at the other girl's arm but she couldn't help laughing. Janice was one on her own, a real original, and she was warm and funny and kind. In the short time she had known her, Essie had found she liked Christine's cousin very much. And Janice was quite right—it was every bit as insulting for Xavier to label Janice as it was for him to label her, Essie thought militantly. Janice might not look like Marilyn Monroe but that didn't mean she couldn't make it in the theatre, or that she didn't have plenty to offer a man.

The two girls did a duty tour of some of the guests before making their way to Christine and Charlie's side as the time approached for the bridal couple to get changed. The reception was due to finish at seven o'clock and Christine and Charlie were catching a train to London, where they were staying overnight before flying to Greece for two weeks.

Christine had brought her suitcase to the hotel and now, as Essie and Janice helped the other girl change in the little room the hotel had provided, there were plenty of giggles and fun. And then Christine was ready, looking lovely in a pale blue stretch-silk dress with a white cotton jacket, and the next few minutes were full of goodbyes and confetti and tears from both the mothers as the newly-weds departed in their taxi.

And all the time, through every moment that had elapsed since she had left Xavier's side, Essie was conscious of a tall, dark figure dominating her thoughts and keeping the host of butterflies in her stomach dancing madly.

Perhaps he knew by now? As the taxi disappeared out of the hotel car park with a cheerful honking of its horn, Essie turned to survey the crowd standing on the steps, and immediately she caught Xavier's eye. He was at least a couple of inches taller than the other men present but it was more the quality of aloofness that seemed to permeate his air space that acted as a magnet. And she saw straight away, from the warm smile and lazily hooded eyes, that as yet he was oblivious to the trick she had played on him.

And Janice was right, he *was* gorgeous, she admitted faintly. The dark grey suit that screamed a designer label, the jade-green shirt and silk tie were all of the very best, but it was him—Xavier Grey—that was breathtaking.

She shouldn't have started this. The thought was there and it was disturbing, but in the next moment he had made his way to her side, looking down at her with silver-blue eyes that caught the last of the dying sunlight.

'You performed your duties admirably.' His smile included Janice, who was standing at her side, and now his gaze swept over the pair of them as he said courteously, 'Perhaps you would allow me to buy you both dinner, if you're not otherwise engaged?'

She must tell him. This had gone far enough and it was time to come clean. But before she could open her mouth Janice said brightly, 'Oh, I'm sorry, Mr Grey, but I'm already booked. I'm sure Janice would love to have dinner with you, though.'

'Would you? Love to have dinner with me, that is?' he asked her softly as Janice disappeared with a cheerful goodbye into the crowd moving back into the hotel.

'I...I don't know—'

'You'd be taking pity on a lonely stranger if you did,' he drawled persuasively. 'I'm booked into a hotel—my own choice, as I'm sure you know. I can't stand these family get-togethers,' he added, somewhat caustically, 'and I'm flying to Germany to oversee a business deal first thing in the morning. I wasn't looking forward to eating alone.'

She doubted that. He was the type of man who would relish being alone—hadn't his own comment confirmed that very thing? And on their tour of the guests earlier Janice had whispered in her ear that Aunt June had told her Charlie's relations had been falling over themselves to persuade him to stay with one of them but he had declined all invitations, graciously but very firmly.

'And I think we might even allow you a couple of glasses of wine,' he continued quietly, blithely unaware of her sudden sharp look at his face, 'if your stomach's recovered?'

'It wasn't a hangover, actually.' Her voice was tight but she couldn't help it—enough was enough. 'I had a touch of food poisoning from a suspect seafood cocktail last night.' He would *allow* her a couple of glasses of wine! What did he think she was? A little puppy being allowed treats?

'Really?' It was lazy and relaxed and told her he didn't believe a word of it, and it made her mad. Even more mad than she had felt earlier.

'Yes, really,' she said bitingly, and this time he noticed the tone.

'Don't be prickly, Janice. I'm only thinking of you,' he said softly, 'and there's nothing worse than a woman who doesn't know when she'd had enough. It's most…unattractive.'

She'd had enough, all right—more than enough—and the façade was back on with a vengeance! He wanted a cute little girlie to keep him company tonight, did he? Well, he was going to get just a little more than he had bargained for.

She took a long deep breath, a *really* long deep breath, and prayed for the strength to control her anger and not blow it. 'I'd love to have dinner with you, Xavier,' she said carefully.

'Good.' His voice was slightly amused; he clearly thought she was still a little huffy. 'I'll pick you up from your home, shall I? What's the address?'

'Oh, no, don't do that.' What did she say now? What excuse could she give? Her mind had gone blank. Essie thought frantically, and then said quickly, 'I've got to see a couple of

college friends about a project we're involved
in, first. I'll get a taxi to your hotel after I'm
through—say, about eight-thirty? Is that
okay?'

'Sure.' His eyes had narrowed slightly but
the tone was still relaxed. 'I'm staying at the
Blue Baron. Do you know it?'

Did she know it? She was staying there herself! Essie smiled and prayed some more, this
time for the ability to hide her agitation from
those razor-sharp eyes that had homed in on
her with unnerving perception.

'Yes, I know it.' She heard her voice speak
calmly and coolly and was amazed at how normal it sounded. Perhaps she *had* gone in for
the wrong career, after all; she was better at
this acting than she would ever have thought
possible! 'Till eight-thirty, then.'

'Eight-thirty.' And then he bent his head towards her, his gaze mesmerising as it held
hers. Although she knew he was going to kiss
her and that she really should pull back, she
didn't.

His lips were warm and firm as they brushed
hers in the lightest of caresses, and he turned
away immediately, but not before she had felt
a hundred tiny electric shocks tingle in every

nerve in her body. They were still tingling, warm and fluid, as she watched him make his goodbyes to the two respective pairs of parents, before striding down into the car park and over to a dark blue Mercedes.

He didn't look at her again as he drove out of the hotel grounds but she knew he was aware of her—as vitally aware of her as she was of him. And again she told herself this was crazy, dangerous, that she was way, way out of her league and that her little joke, her small effort at revenge, had escalated into something more disturbing.

Janice joined her as the Mercedes disappeared, tucking her arm through Essie's as she said, 'You're seeing him tonight?' in a tone that said she knew the answer before Essie spoke.

Essie nodded slowly.

'Then take it from me, girl, tell him in the first few seconds what you've done, turn it into a joke against yourself somehow, and you'll have him eating out of your hand. He's crazy about you; he fancies you like mad.'

'He fancies Janice Beaver, actually,' Essie said, with a weak smile.

'A rose by any other name...' Janice grinned at her before she said again, urgently this time, 'Tell him, Essie, right off. That way you can start again, and who knows what might come of it?'

'I don't want anything to come of it.'

'No?' Janice's tone was sceptical.

'No. I mean it.' Essie turned to look Janice full in the face now, and something in her eyes made Janice's gaze narrow. 'The last thing I want to do is to get involved in a relationship, Janice. There was someone at university... Well, I got my fingers badly burned, that's all, and I prefer the odd light date with no strings attached now. My career is my life and I intend to keep it that way.'

'You sound a perfect match for Xavier, if you ask me.' Janice looked into the ethereally beautiful face that was quite strikingly lovely for a few moments before she murmured, 'Yes, the perfect match.'

CHAPTER TWO

ESSIE felt ridiculously like an escaped convict on the run or some other kind of ne'er-do-well as she skulked back into the Blue Baron half an hour after Xavier had left the wedding reception, keeping an eye out for a tall dark Canadian as she did so.

She had grilled Janice on all the other girl knew about Xavier Grey before she had said goodbye, but had learnt little more than Janice had already told her. Christine's cousin had said that Xavier's branch of Charlie's family had moved out to Canada before Xavier was born, but apparently Xavier had business links in England. And he was a self-made man; Janice had been quite emphatic on that point. A rags-to-riches story, by all accounts, she'd told Essie quietly, although her aunt June—the fount of all knowledge—hadn't had any details.

Once in her hotel room, Essie sank down onto the bed, throwing herself back against the pillows as she contemplated the evening ahead with a groan.

At least she didn't have to consider what she was going to wear, she thought ruefully. She had only brought a pair of jeans and jumper, a casual day dress and one cocktail number with her, knowing she was only staying over-night. And the first two options were definitely not suitable for a date with Xavier Grey! She groaned again, rolling over onto her face and burying her head in the pillows.

She'd been looking forward to a nice re-laxed evening in her room, courtesy of room service and the TV—the train journey up from Sussex had meant an excruciatingly early start, to arrive at Christine's parents' home mid-morning—and now, due to her own foolish-ness, she admitted reluctantly, she was com-mitted to an encounter that would be neither nice nor relaxed! She didn't dare to consider Xavier's reaction when she told him who she really was.

Still, she wasn't sorry. She jerked herself upright, walked over to the full-length mirror in one corner of the room and looked at the reflection that stared out at her. The deep blue eyes were stormy and her soft, full mouth was pulled tight, and now she threw back the mass of gold curls that had escaped the knot she had bundled them into on leaving the wedding reception, and surveyed herself critically.

Okay, so she was slender and not particularly tall, and her colouring and physical appearance might not be the most robust for a veterinary surgeon, but she was damn good at her job—as she was proving every day at the small practice in Sussex where she worked. Brute strength wasn't everything. She scowled at the image in the mirror. And even if the majority of the practice's cases were domestic there were still some occasions when the animals were pretty ferocious, like that Great Dane a few weeks ago that had objected to being examined. The owner had all but disappeared and she had been left facing a gigantic pair of jaws that stated quite clearly its anal glands were its own concern.

She smiled at the memory, in spite of herself. She was fond of Monty and normally the massive Great Dane was putty in her hands, but he had suffered a number of undignified examinations in quick succession due to his problem and, that particular day, he had decided he had to assert himself.

Still, she'd rather take on ten Montys than one Xavier Grey. The thought dimmed her smile and straightened her mouth again.

A bath. She needed a few relaxed moments in a hot bath. She glanced at her watch and saw she had another forty-five minutes before zero hour. And after her bath she'd moisturise and paint and titivate herself and try to work up some sort of courage for the night ahead.

At exactly half-past eight, when Essie walked out of the lift into the reception area of the Blue Baron, she looked every inch the elegant, sophisticated woman of the world and not at all like the young, girlish bridesmaid she had seemed earlier.

The reasons for this were manifold—one, the delicate, up-swept hairstyle that confined her curls in an exquisite arrangement at the back of her head, allowing the long sweep of her neck its true grace. Two, her careful make-up, tasteful and refined, that enhanced the allure of her deep blue eyes and creamy clear skin. Three, the *savoir-faire* of her chic cocktail dress in midnight-blue silk with matching jacket—bought at a Sussex clothes shop which specialised in couturier, nearly-new clothes at a fraction of the original price. Four, her determination that she was going to match Xavier Grey every inch of the way tonight and leave, if not in a blaze of glory, then at least with her head held high.

And there were more reasons, some of which Essie was only faintly aware of herself, that were steeling her backbone and putting iron resolve in her spirit.

She had thought the fact that she emerged from the lift inside the hotel would preclude any further misunderstanding between them as to her identity, and that might well have been the case if Xavier hadn't been deep in conversation with one of the hotel reception staff and missed her appearance.

As it was, he raised his head just in time to see her almost at his side, and she caught the flash of surprise in the silver-blue eyes just before he said, 'Janice, I'm so pleased you could come. Our table is booked for nine but perhaps you would care for a cocktail first?'

A cocktail—the giddy empty-head was being allowed a cocktail, was she? 'Thank you.' She was all coolness and aplomb tonight and she knew it had thrown him. 'That would be lovely.'

He led her into the hotel cocktail lounge
with his hand at her elbow, and she tried not
to think about how delicious he had looked in
that first moment she had seen him. He had
dressed up, as had she, and the black dinner
suit and snowy-white shirt and bow-tie had
made her heart pound. It was still pounding. It
didn't seem as if it would ever *stop* pounding.

'What would you like?'

As she perched elegantly on one of the bar
stools, she allowed a full ten seconds to pass
by before she glanced his way, and then her
voice was serene and self-possessed when she
said, 'Oh, a gin sling I think.'

'A good choice; I'll join you.'

Once he had given the order to the bar-
tender—a Tom Cruise look-alike—Xavier
turned the full intensity of his ice-blue gaze on
her as he said, his voice thoughtful, 'You look
different tonight, Janice. Older, more...
cosmopolitan.'

'Do I?' She arched her eyebrows at him but
there was going to be no batting of eyelashes
tonight. Tonight she was going to be every
inch the twenty-eight-year-old, career-minded,
strong woman she really was! 'Well, I've
never thought first impressions were the best

to go by, Xavier.' She smiled coolly. 'They can be so misleading, don't you think?'

'On occasion.' The narrowed gaze eyed her contemplatively.

Did he know how it made him look when he half shut his eyes like that? Essie asked herself silently. His maleness was emphasised a hundred times, bringing a rawness to his attractiveness that was a killer. But of course he knew! She answered the unspoken question in the next breath, her thoughts astringent. It was all part of the grand seduction scene. She had told herself in the first moments of meeting him that Xavier Grey wouldn't conduct a liaison in the back seat of his car, and how right she had been. First the dinner, then the hotel room—she'd read him like an open book.

'What's the matter?' Xavier asked with an abruptness that took Essie by surprise.

'The matter?' she prevaricated uneasily.

'What made you look like that just then?'

Oh, help; oh, help. She looked back into the strong-boned face and she saw the cleanly sculpted mouth and square jaw were set in stubborn mode. He wasn't going to be diverted, the body language was quite clear, but suddenly everything in Essie rebelled as un-

welcome memories of another strong man—
who had all but broken her heart and her
spirit—came rushing in.

'Nothing.' She raised her chin as she spoke
and met the silver-blue gaze head-on. 'I'm absolutely fine.' Then, as the barman produced
two frosted fluted glasses, she turned to the
young man gratefully, her voice laughing as
she said, 'Wow. Now that's what I call a cocktail.'

'And it will taste as good as it looks,
ma'am.' The good-looking face smiled back at
her, frankly appreciative of the beauty of the
woman in front of him. He had all sorts in his
bar during the average week, but this one was
something special.

'I'm sure it will.' Essie dimpled at him and
then sipped at the cocktail. It was strong, and
delicious. 'It's lovely. Thank you,' she said
smilingly.

Xavier had watched the little exchange without saying a word but now he reached for his
own glass and Essie saw his face was expressionless. 'Excellent.' He gave his own com-
mendation to the young man. 'You've got the
mix just right; there are some people who
drown the sloe gin.'

'Not me, sir.' The barman grinned happily before turning away as another customer claimed his attention.

'Shall we?' Xavier indicated a quiet table for two in a corner of the room with a wave of his hand, and Essie slid off the stool reluctantly. It had seemed safer at the bar, if only because it was delaying the inevitable moment when she had to admit her deception.

They were just about to walk across the room when a sudden squeal of delight made Xavier freeze. Essie heard him groan slightly but then, as a tall, elegant redhead and a very good-looking young man with a shock of black hair hailed them from the doorway, he raised a hand in reply. Essie recognised them from the wedding reception but she had no idea who they were—although that was soon rectified as the redhead strode determinedly across to them, dragging her partner with her.

'Xavier, how lovely! Have you eaten yet?' she asked brightly. 'They've just fitted us in for nine.'

'I thought you and Harper were going out with some of the English relatives?' Xavier answered the woman with a question and he didn't bother to hide his irritation.

'We were.' The redhead smiled at Essie as she spoke, her blue eyes frankly curious. 'But Harper didn't feel too well earlier so we decided to give it a miss. He's feeling heaps better now, though, aren't you, darling?'

She smiled up into Harper's face before she continued, 'Aren't you going to introduce us, Xavier?' as she held out her hand to Essie.

'Janice, this is Candy and Harper. Harper and Candy—Janice.' Xavier's tone was very dry as he added, 'Candy is my niece and Harper is her fiancé.'

'Your niece?' Essie tried not to sound surprised but she didn't manage it very well, as Candy's next words indicated.

'I know what you're thinking but my mother, Xavier's sister, had me when she was very young,' Candy said quickly.

Essie smiled and nodded but didn't pursue the conversation. She sensed there was something here that the other girl found difficult and she didn't want to embarrass her; besides which, she was hoping the other two wouldn't join them, even though she had instinctively warmed to Xavier's niece. She had to *tell* him as soon as possible—and an audience was the last thing she needed. He had already introduced her as Janice, as it was, and now she was feeling acutely uncomfortable and more than a little guilty.

There was a moment or two of silence and then Xavier said, his tone resigned, 'Would you care to join us for an aperitif?'

'If that's all right?' Candy's tone was subdued now; she had obviously clicked onto the fact that her uncle was less than pleased to see them.

'Of course it is.' Essie's voice was warm. There was something almost vulnerable about Xavier's niece; Essie couldn't quite explain it, but she felt that behind the lovely façade of clear translucent skin, vivid blue eyes and wonderful chestnut-red hair the other girl wasn't quite so confident as she appeared, and Essie forgot all her previous thoughts about being alone with Xavier as she aimed to make the young couple feel welcome.

And so it continued through the evening. When they all walked through into the restaurant, it seemed natural for Candy and Harper to join them, especially as their tables were next to each other and only took a moment to put together.

The meal was wonderful, all five courses of it, the wine undoubtedly expensive, and Xavier was an excellent host—courteous, amusing and urbane. But behind the cultured, suave exterior Essie sensed he was watching them all in the same way a scientist examined something he found interesting. He gave *nothing* of himself away.

As soon as the thought hit, she knew it was the truth. Xavier was the epitome of the cool, controlled ice-man, however light and witty his conversation, and however much that sexy, sensual mouth smiled. *Sexy and sensual?* She caught herself up sharply, irritated she'd noticed. He wasn't sexy or sensual or anything else—he was simply the enemy, as far as she was concerned, and she'd better remember that. Once she'd told him—if they ever got to be alone for a moment or two—it would be wise to beat a hasty retreat. This was not a man to mess with.

They lingered over their liqueur coffees—the rich, brandy-flavoured coffee topped with whipped cream was the best Essie had tasted and the pianist who had been playing a medley of songs while the diners ate was excellent—but then, after Xavier had insisted the meal was his treat to Harper, the other two rose to leave.

'Thanks, Xavier.' Candy leant forward and touched her uncle's arm with a smile.

Essie found herself asking—although she hadn't meant to, 'You don't call him Uncle, then?'

'Uncle?' Candy grinned. 'With only ten years between us? Besides, I've never thought of Xavier as an uncle; he's the big brother I never had.' There was real affection in the lovely blue eyes and, as Xavier glanced at his niece, Essie saw a softness to his smile she hadn't seen before. And it hurt. Ridiculously, irrationally, it hurt like mad, because she knew he would never look at her like that. In fact, once she told him the truth, she didn't dare to think how he would look.

But she didn't *want* him to look at her like that, anyway! Good grief, it was the last thing she wanted! What on earth was she thinking of? The protests came, fierce and strong, and such was her agitation that she let her napkin slip under the table so she could bend down and retrieve it and compose her face again.

She loathed his type of man! She loathed *him*; he was a typical male chauvinist with a

grossly exaggerated idea of himself. Okay, so
this evening had been fun—she had to admit
she'd enjoyed herself, in spite of everything—
but that was because he was in entertainment
mode, that was all. The real man was still
there, under the façade of smooth dinner com-
panion. He was a control freak, like the rest of
his kind.

Essie had accepted a brandy when the other
two had declined—not because she wanted
one, but because it would give her an opportunity to talk to Xavier with other people
around, and she had the feeling she would
need their unsuspecting support. And now, as
Xavier settled back into his chair, his powerful
chest muscles flexing under the thin white silk
of his shirt—the jacket long since discarded on
the back of his chair—she took a quick sip of
the fine thirty-year-old spirit as she contemplated how to start.

'Don't you ever relax?'

'What?' The deep, husky voice had been
very soft and now Essie stared straight at him,
her eyes narrowing warily. This was the start
of the seduction programme, was it? The one
that had been put on hold when his niece and
her fiancé had joined them so unexpectedly.

'You've been on edge all evening. I could almost feel the waves coming off you,' he drawled lazily, 'and you were the same this afternoon, but in a different way.'

He was too perceptive by half. She watched his eyes wander over her face and she knew he was doing it deliberately, his gaze pausing on the soft swell of her lips until she could feel them tingle as though he had kissed her.

'I don't know what you mean,' she said tightly. She was going to tell him, she *was*, but in her own way, and certainly not defending herself at the same time.

'You're like several different women under the same skin,' he said thoughtfully, 'and you change from one to the other like a nervous little chameleon. Why are you so guarded to-night, Janice? Is it me in particular you're chary of, or all men?'

This had gone quite far enough and, in view of his comments, there would never be a better opportunity to tell him he had made a mis-take—a big mistake—this afternoon, she thought feverishly. And then he completely took the wind out of her sails and had her floundering for words when he leant forward, his hard dark face amazingly tender, and said,

'You're a phoney, Janice Beaver. All this wild living and seeking of attention—that's not the real girl. Has someone hurt you? Is that it? Whatever he did, whatever happened, he's not worth messing up your life for. Believe me, I know.'

'Xavier, please.' This was awful, terrible. He was making her feel so guilty. She took a deep breath, her nostrils flaring, and removed her hand from where it was resting under his before she said, 'This isn't like you think.'

'Someone *did* hurt you, didn't they?' It was as though he hadn't heard her. 'And badly.'

She wished she'd never started this. She swallowed deeply, the tension making her voice brittle as she said, 'That's nothing to do with this and it was a long time ago.'

'Time's relative and it might help to talk about it.'

She had to explain who she was. She took another deep breath, the elusive and very male scent of him teasing her nostrils as he leant even closer, his silvery eyes reflecting a shaft of light from the discreetly placed lamp above their table, and she had just opened her mouth to begin, to *tell* him, when the pianist stopped playing and instead spoke into his microphone, reading from a card one of the waiters had just given him.

'Sorry to interrupt the flow, ladies and gentlemen, but there is an urgent call for Miss Esther Russell. If Miss Russell is here, perhaps she would make her presence known or make her way to Reception.'

'Janice?' Xavier's voice brought her startled eyes back to his. 'Don't let him win, don't let him ruin your life, because that's what'll happen if you're not careful.'

'I have to go to Reception.' Essie's voice was slightly hysterical but she couldn't believe this was happening. It was like a black comedy, a dark farce.

'Reception?' And then his brows drew together as he said, 'Esther Russell? Isn't that the girl you were bridesmaid with today? Is she in the hotel, then? Do you know where she is?'

'She—she is me,' Essie stammered ungrammatically.

'She's you?' He stared at her as though she had lost her mind and maybe she had, Essie thought wildly. Perhaps that explained why she had been so incredibly stupid as to think she could take Xavier Grey on and win.

'Look, I must answer that call.' She rose as she spoke and he rose with her, his manners impeccable even in the midst of all the confusion. 'Please, you stay here.' She couldn't have him standing over her while she spoke into the telephone; she wouldn't be coherent. 'I'll be back in a few moments, I promise, and then I'll explain properly, but…but I'm Esther Russell and the call is probably to do with my work and it'll be important. I…I have to go.'

He nodded, somehow giving the impression that he hadn't moved a muscle at the same time, and she gave him one last helpless look before fairly flying out of the restaurant.

Oh, it couldn't have all gone more wrong, she told herself frantically as she hurried over to the reception desk, and what on earth was this call about? It could only be Jamie or Peter, and they would never have bothered her unless there was some sort of disaster—but for the life of her she couldn't think what.

'Essie?' It was Peter Hargreaves, who owned the small town practice where she worked, and his voice was both apologetic and frustrated. 'Essie, I'm sorry to bother you on your weekend off and at this time of night, but it's urgent. That case you've been dealing with, Colonel Llewellyn's hunter? Well, the horse has taken a turn for the worse and I think I need to operate, but I can't find the case history. The animal's worth a fortune and you know how much the Colonel thinks of him— he treats him better than he does his wife, and I dare not leave anything to chance. I need to be fully acquainted with everything you've done so far and the strengths of the medication he's on, all of it. The damn computer's down and I can't find the hard-copy file. Any ideas?'

Essie wrinkled her brow. They rarely bothered with the hard-copy files—Peter had an excellent computer system that was both efficient and fast—but there was always the odd occasion, like this one, when old methods came into their own.

'It's not in the filing cabinet, obviously, else you wouldn't be ringing me.' Essie thought for a moment. 'Have you asked Jamie if he knows?'

'He's out at Sanderson's farm: his daughter's pony's sick, and you know old man Sanderson. He must be the one person in the whole of creation not to own a phone,' Peter said tersely. 'Silly old blighter. It's a hell of a way there, with the Colonel's place in the opposite direction, and I might miss Jamie anyway.'

'You say he's gone to deal with Jenny Sanderson's pony?' Essie asked quickly.

'Yes. It sounded like it had colic, which was what we thought the Colonel's hunter had, but—'

Essie thought rapidly. She knew Jamie's habit of slinging every scrap of paper that ever came his way into the huge bottom drawer of his desk until it became too full to close—it didn't matter what it was: letters, cheques, circulars, reports—they all went in. 'Could Jamie have got the Colonel's file out before he went to the Sanderson farm?' she asked carefully. 'If the symptoms were similar, he might have checked that file first, in case it proved the two cases were linked.'

'You think he's taken the damn file with him?' her boss growled furiously.

She hoped not, oh, she did hope not, because Jamie had been in hot water more than once lately for his cavalier attitude to paperwork and records.

Essie crossed her fingers and said rapidly, 'I'm sure he hasn't but he might have looked at it and, if he was in a hurry to get to the farm, put it in the bottom drawer of his desk for quickness until he got back.'

'He'd better not have, not with the computer down. Hang on a minute, Essie, and I'll check.'

The silence at the other end of the telephone made Essie aware of her surroundings again and, as she glanced across the thickly carpeted, luxurious reception area towards the big glass doors through which the restaurant was located, she felt her stomach turn right over. Xavier was going to be mad. He was going to be absolutely livid, she told herself weakly.

'Essie?' It was Peter's voice again and now she jerked her attention back to the matter in hand. 'I've got it. The young fool's got everything but the kitchen sink in that drawer. You wouldn't believe it.'

She would.

There was the sound of rustling paper and then Peter said, 'Yep, I can see exactly what you've done and it's fine, just fine. Right, I'll take it from here and I'm really sorry to have bothered you, Essie. How did the wedding go?'

It was very much an afterthought and Peter was clearly anxious to get out to the Colonel's place, so Essie kept her answer brief. 'Very well, thanks, Peter. Look, I shan't leave till about ten in the morning, so if you need me at any time before then, please ring. Okay?'

'Thanks, Essie, but I'll be fine now I've got the records. Jamie's a damn good vet but he's going to have to pull his socks up in certain areas.' There was a brief pause and then he said, 'Goodbye for now. You carry on enjoying yourself and I'll see you on Monday.'

'All right, Peter. Goodnight.'

Enjoying herself. Essie stood for a moment more before she put the telephone down and thanked the receptionist. Enjoying herself wasn't quite the term she would have used...

Xavier's dark presence seemed to fill the whole restaurant when Essie stepped back into the quiet surroundings some moments later. It all looked the same—the pianist was still playing, the other diners were quietly enjoying the excellent food, the odd hum of conversation and genteel laugh adding to the overall gentle ambience of the hushed room; but there, in the distance, was Xavier.

She hardly knew how to walk as she approached their table; she was vitally aware of the narrowed gaze trained on her face and the grimness that was reflected in every line of his big frame, but then she was sliding into her seat and looking straight into the icy countenance.

'Well?' One word—but more telling than any tirade.

'I'm sorry.' It was little more than a whisper.

'Not good enough. Not nearly good enough.' He stared at her for a moment more before saying, his voice biting, 'You're telling me *you* are Esther Russell, have I got that straight? Which means you are Christine's best friend, not her cousin, and you're a veterinary surgeon?' The tone held a note of incredulity even the cold rage couldn't quite hide, and that, more than anything else, put steel in Essie's backbone. He *still* thought it was virtually impossible that she was an intelligent, successful and capable human being, she thought furiously.

'Yes, that's right.' Her head was up and her chin was out and further thoughts of apology were out of the question.

'So how old are you?' he asked tightly.

'Twenty-eight.' It was a little snap. And then, before he could say anything else, she added, 'And all this wouldn't have happened if you hadn't been so darn rude.'

'*What?*' His bark brought a number of heads turning towards their table and, as Xavier became aware of the attention and glared back at the unfortunate diners, heads were quickly lowered to their plates. 'I really don't believe you just said that,' he growled savagely. 'You spin me a pack of lies and then you tell me it's *my* fault?'

'I didn't spin you a pack of lies, not really,' Essie shot back quickly. 'You came to me, remember, and stated a number of things before I even opened my mouth. You assumed I was Janice; you lectured me on my lifestyle, my morals, *everything*, and we hadn't even been introduced!'

'You *lied* to me.'

'I merely went along with your assumptions, that's all. And, while we're on the subject, they were pretty insulting,' Essie said bitterly. 'You looked at Janice and you looked at me, and in your mind there was no doubt about which of the two bridesmaids was the hopeful budding actress leading a somewhat wild lifestyle. You hadn't spoken to either of us, you didn't know us from Adam, and yet you labelled me a dumb little blonde. Right or wrong?'

'This is crazy!' Dark colour flared across the hard cheekbones and Essie had never seen someone look so furious in all her life. There was certainly no vestige of the cool, controlled ice-man left, she thought somewhat hysterically. The man in front of her was positively smouldering with fury.

'Right or wrong?' she ground out determinedly, refusing to be intimidated, even though her stomach was churning and her hands were damp with perspiration.

'Wrong,' he snarled grimly. 'If I had thought you were just a dumb little blonde, I wouldn't have asked you out tonight.'

'Whatever you say, however you try and turn this round, you know full well I'm right,' Essie said proudly, staring right back into the angry male face as she forced her fear and panic back down into the hidden depths of her. 'I admit I shouldn't have continued what you started—' here Xavier, who had just taken a swig of his brandy, nearly choked '—but it was too good an opportunity to miss, if you want the truth.'

'The truth? You don't know the meaning of the word.'

'Actually, I do.' Violet-blue eyes held iced silver and neither would give way. Essie was conscious of the cry deep inside her that was saying she hadn't *wanted* it to be like this, that she should have told him before, should have set things straight as soon as she had seen him tonight to prevent just such an occurrence as this; but it was too late now for regrets. 'I'm a very honest person normally, but your arrogance annoyed me, if you want to know.'

'My arrogance?' he ground out with dangerous calm.

He looked as though he couldn't believe his ears and perhaps he couldn't, Essie thought faintly; it was quite likely no one had ever spoken to him like this in his life.

'Yes, your arrogance,' she said a little shakily. 'You were pompous and high-handed and unforgivably rude, and you had absolutely no right to assume anything about me—or Janice, if it comes to that. I've worked hard to get where I am, Xavier Grey. No one has given me anything *ever*, but I'm a damn good vet. And I don't appreciate any label—whatever it is—by someone who doesn't know me. Is that clear?'

'Abundantly.'

He had settled back in his seat during her quietly spoken tirade, the laser-sharp gaze assessing the angry young woman in front of him, and now the cool, sardonic tinge to his voice was incredibly galling.

'And you can cut the lordly disdain,' Essie fired back angrily, 'because it doesn't wash with me. I don't care how rich or how powerful you are—you're still ill-mannered and presumptuous and—'

'You're going to run out of adjectives before long,' he said expressionlessly, his face now betraying nothing of what he was thinking. And the discipline he had brought into play, the regaining of that icy control and cool restraint, told Essie she had to get out of there fast before she further compounded her sins by flinging the contents of her brandy glass straight into that implacable countenance.

'Goodbye, Mr. Grey.' She rose abruptly, her face as white as a sheet but her voice firm. 'And I shall settle the account for my own dinner, thank you.'

'Now you're being boorish.' It was a soft, low Canadian drawl and had Essie's hands clenching at her sides as her innate British sense of propriety warred with the red-hot desire to see Xavier Grey with brandy dripping off the end of his nose. The natural reserve won, but it was a close thing.

Essie was very aware of the subdued interest of the surrounding tables as she turned to leave, but it was the silver- blue eyes boring into the middle of her back that kept her stride measured and controlled as she left the restaurant with her head held high.

The control held until she reached her room, but, once she had closed the door behind her, she sank down onto the thick blue carpet. Her legs refused to hold her any longer.

How could she have said all that? She pressed her hands to her burning cheeks as she swayed back and forth in a little heap on the floor. Not that he hadn't deserved it—he had—but she wasn't normally like this, for goodness' sake. He brought out the very worst in her, she reflected miserably. In fact, there was a whole side of her nature that had seemed to develop over the last few hours that was positively alarming.

She continued to sit for a few moments more, leaning back against the door as her mind went over every word and action that had happened below in the restaurant. And then she leapt up from the floor, walking over to the telephone and picking it up with a hand that trembled slightly.

'Hello, is that Reception?' She gave her room number before continuing, 'I ate in the restaurant tonight along with another party under the name of Grey, but I'd like my meal to be put on my own account. Is that possible?' She gave the details, thanked the receptionist and then put down the phone abruptly.

What a mess. She shook her head slowly. And it all seemed to have developed so quickly. She hadn't known Xavier Grey existed before today, but now she doubted if she would ever forget him in the whole of her life. The next thought brought a wry, reluctant smile—he would probably remember her for quite some time, too!

She was wound up as tightly as a coiled spring, she decided irritably as she pulled off the beautiful jacket and dress. She'd never sleep like this. She frowned at the golden-haired figure in the mirror and pulled out the pins from the intricate hairstyle with savage haste.

She'd do her packing now, ready for an early start in the morning, then have a long, hot, scented bath and wash her hair.

Nearly an hour and a half later, after she'd soaked until she was in danger of resembling a wrinkled prune and washed and dried her hair, Essie sat on the big soft bed in her room and sighed. Sleep was a million miles away— it was almost one o'clock in the morning—and she should be zonked out cold after the sort of exhausting day she'd had.

But thoughts of a big dark Canadian were keeping the adrenalin pulsing through her body like liquid fire. She didn't want to see him again. She sucked in her bottom lip as she con- templated his face in the last few minutes she had been with him and shivered, in spite of the hothouse warmth of the hotel room. She'd *die* if she had to see him again! And there was breakfast. Would he be in the dining room? Of course, she could always ring down now and ask for breakfast to be served in her room, but there was the checking out, too. He might be there then.

Oh, don't be such a wimp! The thought was hot and vitriolic and she screwed up her face against it. She could handle Xavier Grey; she'd handled Colin Fulton, hadn't she? And survived the aftermath of finishing with Andrew at university. Funny how the two men were always connected in her mind. Or perhaps it wasn't so funny, if she thought about it. The first—her stepfather—had left her a sitting duck for the attention of the latter.

But she wasn't going to think of all that now. She straightened her face and opened her eyes, reaching for the phone again as she did so. She would call down to Reception and ask them to get her bill ready very early, and then she'd skip breakfast and catch the first train home. This was an unfortunate episode in her life but that was all it was; she was still in control.

She nodded to herself, ignoring the tremble in her stomach that accompanied the shadow of a tall dark man with ice-blue eyes that could resemble soft liquid silver when they wanted to, and a harsh mouth that had been tender and caring in the last few minutes before he had found out who she really was.

But she didn't want Xavier Grey to be tender or caring anyway, she told herself sternly in the next moment. A man like him—rich, powerful, magnetic, with women in their busloads chasing after him—wouldn't look twice at a little nobody like her. She didn't have the right connections, the right friends, and she didn't have a clue what went on in his world. And she didn't want to. He had wanted her purely in a physical sense. If she had been who he thought she was, he'd intended to sleep with her tonight; she just knew it. A quick one-night stand to spice up what he'd found a boring duty; that was all she had meant to him.

Well, this was one cute little cookie who had turned out a darn sight tougher than he'd expected. The thought brought no comfort and that made her even more confused and disturbed. No, she *definitely* didn't want to run into Xavier Grey again, she affirmed more strongly, and she would make sure she didn't.

End of story.

CHAPTER THREE

'AND you're telling me you hightailed it out of the hotel without ever seeing this poor guy again? You didn't even write him a note to say you were sorry?'

Was he winding her up or something? Essie stared at Jamie frowningly, her mouth tight. 'He wasn't a ''poor guy'', Jamie—I told you,' she said coolly. 'And neither did I ''hightail'' it anywhere.'

'No?'

'*No!*'

'All right, all right.' Jamie held up his hands in surrender, and then, as she continued to glare at him, he said quietly, 'It's just that all this is so unlike you, Essie.'

Essie frowned a moment more before she sighed deeply, relaxing as she said, 'Oh, I know it is, Jamie. I suppose that's why I had to tell you about it—because I feel a bit guilty deep down. But he *was* arrogant, terribly so, and so...'

73

'What?' Jamie's nice, pleasant, freckled face topped by its shock of ginger hair was enquiring.

Essie shrugged. She didn't know how to explain the unexplainable and she wished she'd never mentioned this to Jamie now. She wouldn't have, except for the fact that they were both reeling on their toes from Peter's shock announcement that morning that he was going to sell the practice and emigrate, and when Jamie had suggested the two of them have lunch together and discuss their options she'd agreed. And then, once that subject had been exhausted, Jamie had asked about the wedding the week before, and—with her defences momentarily down—she'd gone and blurted out the whole sorry story.

'Anyway, that's over and done with and we've enough problems in the present to worry over.'

Jamie nodded dismally. He had joined the practice a year before Essie, and they had both thought their jobs were secure. Peter Hargreaves had taken over from the old vet— who had owned the practice for donkey's years—twelve months before he had appointed Jamie, and he had transformed it from the rather run-down, one-man show it had been in those days to the enterprising, modern business it was today.

And Peter had intended to make the practice his life's work—he'd told them that at their respective interviews—but now it appeared he'd had an offer he couldn't refuse from a veterinary friend in New Zealand to join his practice as a partner, and the prospects for himself and his wife and their young family were too good to pass by.

To date, apparently, Peter had had one firm offer for the business but it was from an older veterinary surgeon who intended to bring his two sons with him—both vets themselves—if he bought the practice. Because of that, and what it would mean to Jamie and Essie, Peter had hesitated, but now time was pressing and he felt he couldn't prevaricate any longer.

'What will you do?' Jamie asked mournfully. 'It'll mean moving to another part of the country, I should think.'

Essie nodded slowly. She'd already thought of that, and the prospect of leaving her beautiful little cottage—the first home she had ever had—was even worse than losing her job. But the possibility of another post right on the doorstep was practically nil. 'I suppose we'd better start looking.' She forced a bright smile for Jamie's benefit. He had just got engaged to a local girl so this was worse, if anything, for him.

The walk back to the surgery from the old-fashioned brass-and-beamed pub was usually one that Essie enjoyed, but today she didn't focus on the tree-lined road and large, prosperous houses this particular part of the town boasted, and there was none of the usual carefree banter with Jamie.

It was as they turned into the wide pebbled drive that led up to the sprawling detached house that was the practice—Peter having converted the top of the premises to a three-bedroomed flat when he and his family had moved in—that Essie stopped stock-still.

Jamie walked on a good few paces before he realised she wasn't with him. 'What?' As he turned and saw her face, he hastily retraced his steps. 'What's the matter, Essie?'

She couldn't answer him for a moment, the sight of the large dark blue Mercedes parked regally in front of the steps leading to the front door had taken her breath away. But it needn't be his, she reassured herself feverishly in the next moment. There must be hundreds of dark blue Mercedes about and she hadn't noticed the numberplate that afternoon at the wedding reception. She glanced at it now—XJG 1—and her heart pounded.

'That car…'

'Beauty, isn't it?' Jamie said covetously.

'I think it's his—the man I told you about,' Essie whispered weakly, the quiet slumberous warmth of the lovely late May afternoon mocking her panic.

'No, he wouldn't bother to try and trace you, Essie.' Jamie had been looking at the car but now he turned back to face her, his puppy-dog eyes taking in the beauty of the slender, lovely young woman in front of him, and as he remembered the long, frustrated nights and achingly painful days he had endured before he had come to terms with the fact that Essie would never look twice at him in *that* way his voice was less certain as he added, 'Would he?'

'He might.' Shock had turned Essie's eyes to midnight-blue. 'Yes, yes, he would. It's just the sort of thing he'd do.'

'Well, you can't stand out here all afternoon,' Jamie said reasonably, 'and we've got

to prepare for the afternoon surgery. Come on.
You don't know for sure it's him, anyway.'

She did and it was.

'Essie.' As she and Jamie stepped into the
hall, Peter appeared like magic at the top of
the stairs. 'Could you spare a moment? There's
someone here to see you.'

Xavier had obviously already worked his
spell on her boss, Essie thought grimly. Peter
wasn't usually so affable and benign with un-
announced visitors, and she had yet to know
of one who was allowed into the holy of holies
of his home. Peter guarded his privacy zeal-
ously and she had only been admitted upstairs
once—and that had been for a Christmas drink,
with Jamie.

She mounted the stairs in the same way
Marie Antoinette must have mounted the steps
to the guillotine, and was ushered into Peter's
very pleasant green and lemon lounge with a
nonchalant sweep of his arm.

'I'll leave you two alone for a moment or
two. I need to speak to Jamie about those cows
with stasis of the rumen. It turns out one of
the farmhands had left a few sacks of turnips
in the yard, damn idiot. And why he couldn't

have told us when we were over there this morning I don't know…'

Peter had shut the door behind him even as he'd still been speaking, and now Essie stood in the middle of the room, looking at the tall, muscular man who had risen to his feet at her entrance.

'You prefer Essie to Esther?' It was the same deep, husky voice that had haunted her dreams for nights, and she had to force herself not to shiver as the impact of it trickled over her taut nerves.

He looked wonderful. The thought was unwelcome in the circumstances. And she must look a real mess—she hadn't had time to do more than wash her hands and comb her hair after a morning spent tramping about smelly outbuildings, ministering to a herd of sick bovines. There was dirt on her jeans and sweatshirt, and she knew the faint odour of cows still clung to her.

Xavier Grey's cold, chiselled face was expressionless but, behind the imperturbable mask, his thoughts were racing. She was even more lovely than he remembered. Standing there, her glorious mass of hair screwed into a high ponytail and her face free of make-up, she

was breathtaking. And she *still* didn't look like
the average veterinary surgeon, damn it!

'Everyone calls me Essie.' She was amazed
at how steady her voice sounded, considering
what she was feeling like inside.

'And you don't mind?'

'Why should I?'

Essie didn't suit her: she was too fragile, too
beautiful to be called that. Esther was the
Persian name for Star; he'd looked it up in the
week—secretly, he admitted ruefully to himself, and anyone who knew him would have a
field day at his expense, if they thought he'd
got it this bad—and the elusive, shining perfection of a star suited her perfectly. But in
view of her touchiness on the subject of her
appearance he didn't think he'd better say so.
It was an unusual experience for Xavier Grey
to watch what he said and he found he didn't
like it. It made his voice curt as he said, 'No
reason.'

Essie looked at him warily. Why on earth
was he here?

Xavier looked back at her and he was thinking exactly the same thing. She didn't like
him—the understatement of the year—and
they couldn't have got off to a worse start if

they'd tried, so why was he pursuing what was clearly a doomed cause?

'Mr Grey—'

'Xavier, please.'

'I don't know why you're here, but if you're looking to make things awkward for me—'

'Of course I'm not.' It was too sharp, too cutting, but she'd caught him on the raw with her assumption that he was out for blood. Was that what she thought of him? he asked himself silently. He forced his voice into conciliatory mode--with some effort—and added, 'I'm here to apologise, that's all.'

'*You?* Apologise?' Her voice was too high and she desperately tried to backtrack as his eyes iced over. 'There's nothing for you to apologise for,' she added weakly. 'It was me...'

He had to be the most attractive man in the world. The exaggeration—and all the danger-ous connotations it implied—frightened Essie to death as it popped into her mind before she could reject it.

He was dressed simply—no designer suit to-day—but the stone-washed denim shirt and jeans sat on the lean, hard male frame like an advertisement for Levi's, and the Italian leather belt and shoes were undoubtedly hand-made. He still looked every inch the hard, ruth-less millionaire with the world at his feet—he probably would even if he was stark naked. That contemplation was totally unnerving and utterly daunting, and there was a hectic flush in Essie's cheeks now.

'On the contrary,' Xavier said smoothly. 'I jumped to conclusions I had no right to as-sume—you were quite right on that score—and in doing so I can understand that I precip-itated our...unfortunate misunderstanding. I was intending to say as much the next morn-ing, but you left before I could do so.'

'I had to get back here. There were prob-lems...' Essie waved her hand vaguely and hoped the generalisation would do.

He nodded, his narrowed eyes still tight on her face. 'As I think I mentioned to you, I was booked on a flight to Germany that same morning, and so I was unable to follow up on our acquaintance until now.'

Follow up on our acquaintance? Essie hoped her face was as expressionless as his. This was all so terribly polite!

'Look, I'm in the area for a day or two. Perhaps you'd allow me to take you out for dinner and we can get things straight?' Xavier asked softly. 'If nothing else, I'd like to clear the air, after all that's happened.'

It would be the equivalent of diving head-first into a live volcano, to start something with Xavier Grey. Essie stared at him, her fingers knotting together as she wondered how she could politely refuse the invitation. 'I'm sorry.' She forced a swift smile. 'I'm afraid I'm absolutely overloaded with work at the moment. There's no way I can take an evening out.'

'You do stop to eat, I take it?'

The tone suggested he was well aware of her lunch date with Jamie and now Essie blushed a bright pink, but the brusqueness in his voice added to her resolve. 'Of course.' She could be as icy as him when she wanted to be. 'But lunch is normally snatched *en route* or I take sandwiches. A working day means I'm usually a little grubby about the edges—' she indicated her jeans with a flick of her hand '—and once I'm home and I've had a bath and so on it's very late in the evening, and all I want to do is to relax with a TV dinner or a takeaway.'

'That must leave you very little time for fun.'

Essie couldn't quite gauge the tone of his voice but she knew she didn't like it, and the dryness which spoke of cynicism, disbelief and a hundred other unwelcome implications deepened the hectic colour in her cheeks. Ever since she had met this man, he had done nothing but confront her and call her a liar—and worse—and she was sick of it. 'We aren't all interested in having fun, Mr Grey,' she said with frigid disdain. 'Some of us have to work hard for a living.'

Oh, that sounded so *priggish* she thought in the next instant, and she wasn't a prig—far from it. But he always made her say and do the wrong thing! He was a hateful man and she loathed him.

He stared at her for some fifteen seconds without speaking, his expression unreadable, and then he gave her a smile which could only be described as supercilious and Essie found she wanted to hit him. Oh, how she wanted to hit him!

'All work and no play…' he drawled softly. He didn't have to finish the old saying; Essie was quite aware he was calling her dull and her chin tilted defiantly as her eyes blazed midnight-blue.

'I don't want to be rude,' she said with acid calm, 'but I *am* busy, Mr Grey. If you've said all you came to say, I really do need to get back to the surgery.'

'So you're telling me you won't even have dinner with me, after I've come all this way carrying the olive branch?' he asked coolly. 'Don't you think that's a little...churlish?'

'Churlish?' It was an angry splutter but she checked herself immediately. She would *not* be provoked! 'I thought you said you were in the area for a day or two, anyway?' she reminded him with stinging sweetness. 'I'm sure you'll be far too busy to worry about whether you have dinner with me or not.'

For such a fragile little thing, she had a bite like a cobra. He could see how she'd master even the most ferocious animal, Xavier thought darkly.

'But I want to have dinner with you, Essie.' There was something telling him to get the hell out of there, to walk out and forget he had ever heard the name of Esther Russell, but he ignored it. It had been a long, long time since he had wanted a woman the way he wanted this one, and even longer since he had been refused. He felt the blood surge hotly through his veins at the challenge.

'And what you want you get, is that it?' He was so close she could smell his delicious scent again, and she didn't like what it did to her senses.

'Exactly.' He smiled a smile that wasn't a smile at all.

'Well, not this time!' She didn't really know why she was quite so mad, but she had passed the stage of caution. 'I have to tell you you're the most arrogant, presumptuous, *conceited*—'

'Not a list of my virtues again?' His hand closed round her wrist as he spoke and he had jerked her into him before she could react. The kiss was hard and angry and, for a moment, Essie couldn't believe it was happening; and it was this very disbelief that worked against her because, by the time she could have responded, she was dizzy with desire.

She knew she ought to be affronted, perhaps even afraid of his strength and the power in the hard-muscled arms that were holding her pressed against his body, but those emotions were totally absent. And that was dangerous— very dangerous—but she couldn't help it. Excitement was singing through every nerve and sinew, a heat that was sweet and almost painful causing her to arch against him as the kiss changed to one of dominant persuasion.

Her head had fallen back against his arms and, as his mouth gained greater penetration, she heard herself whimper her pleasure, but even that didn't bring her out of the spell he had woven. She could feel the thud, thud, thud of his heart pounding against his ribcage, the unmistakable thrust of his arousal against the softness of her belly, but she had never been kissed like this before in her life and it took all lucid thought into a whirling maelstrom of exquisite sensation.

She had read about women being swept away by a flood of passion, watched films or TV dramas where some swooning female had been overcome with lustful yearning, but she had never dreamt such emotions were *real*. But this was real. *He* was real, and he was very, very good at this. It made the fumbling, some- times merely irritating but more often than not just unpleasant lovemaking she had permitted with Andrew fade into insignificance. Andrew had called her frigid more than once, when she had stopped his groping hands and wet mouth before things went too far; he had *insisted* she must be frigid. But she wasn't. Xavier Grey had proved that.

His hands had slid under the thin material of her old worn sweatshirt to the warm silk of her stomach, moving up to cup her breasts through the filmy lace of her bra, and she gasped as tiny needles of pleasure pierced her through.

This was wrong, she thought desperately; but then, as he murmured her name against her lips, his voice deep and husky, she arched against him again and it was only the sound of footsteps on the stairs outside leading to the flat that brought her jerking away, flushed and breathless, as she glanced towards the lounge door.

By the time Peter Hargreaves walked into the room, Xavier was standing by the window, looking down into the drive below. As he turned at the other man's entrance, saying, 'This place is in a fine position, Peter; you can see for miles from here,' Essie saw he was the cool, imperturbable tycoon again, totally equanimous, dignified and imposing. And she didn't miss the fact that he and Peter were already on first-name terms, either.

'Grand, isn't it?' Peter barely glanced at her as he made for Xavier's side. 'I shall be sorry to leave, but Carol and I feel New Zealand is too good to turn down and, if we're going to go for it, we need to do it now, while the kids are still so young. We'd prefer their schooling to be uninterrupted.'

Xavier nodded, his eyes piercing her for one moment over the other man's shoulder as they took in her flushed face and slightly bruised mouth, before his attention returned to Peter. 'I think Essie was just leaving but I'd like a word with you before I go, if you've the time?'

'Of course, of course.' Peter was genial. He'd seen the Mercedes and the gold Rolex and he knew wealth when he saw it.

'Goodbye, Essie.' Xavier looked at her again and this time it was crystal-clear he was giving her her marching orders.

She stared back at him for a long moment, hurt pride and outrage at his curt dismissal warring with the desire to flee his presence and lick her wounds in private. That kiss hadn't meant a thing to him—not a thing! He had used it to teach her a lesson, she thought raggedly, that was all, and he had succeeded beyond his wildest expectations. She had offered herself to him on a plate—she had practically *begged* him to take her—and now, he was silently telling her she didn't mean a thing to him and the offer of dinner had been one of politeness, nothing more.

And that was fine—just fine. She drew herself up, her back as straight as a rod and her violet-blue eyes fierce as she said as coldly as she could manage, 'Goodbye, Mr Grey.'

Her tone of voice must have registered with Peter because she was aware of a sudden movement on the perimeter of her vision as her boss turned to look at her, but she was already on the way to the door and she didn't check her stride.

Once on the landing, with the flat door firmly closed, Essie stood for a few seconds, desperately trying to regain her composure. She must have been mad, back in there, it was the only explanation. She shut her eyes tight against the humiliation and shock that had now drained her face of all colour. How *could* she have let Xavier Grey, let *any* man, handle her like that? She'd had some sort of a brainstorm, that was all.

She descended the stairs slowly, fighting the urge to howl like a baby or fly back up there and slap Xavier's face. But neither action was an option. There was no one to blame for this but herself. The truth was as unwelcome as it was inescapable. She had started the whole ridiculous farce in the first place with her sense of injustice and fury, and she had just been put very firmly in her place by an expert.

Essie wasn't aware of when Xavier left, beyond noticing that the Mercedes was still there when she and Jamie started the afternoon surgery and was gone when they finished, but every second of the long afternoon and evening he was at the forefront of her mind, much as she resented the fact.

It was gone seven before she left the practice and by then she was bone-tired and unutterably weary and wishing she had brought her car to work. On fine days, she tended to leave it parked outside her little cottage—the twenty-minute walk to the surgery was a very pleasant one and it woke her up thoroughly in the mornings and relaxed her at night. But tonight every nerve was screaming and all she wanted was a long hot shower.

Nevertheless, when she finally reached the narrow leafy lane that dipped and dived to her tiny, quaint two-up, two- down haven engulfed in honeysuckle and jasmine, the familiar dart of pleasure pierced her mental and physical exhaustion.

The minute dwelling-place had been in a terrible state when she had first seen it—a fiercely reclusive old lady had lived there and the cottage had been rendered practically uninhabitable inside, although the roof and drains had been sound. But months of hard work had transformed the cottage into a charming home, just big enough for one, with a diminutive bathroom and small bedroom upstairs and—once Essie had had a wall knocked down—a combined sitting room and pint-sized kitchen downstairs.

The whole cottage was lilliputian, though it had still cost an arm and a leg by the time the last lick of paint had been applied; but the garden was something else. It measured almost a third of an acre and had been the old lady's pride and joy, from the wonderful old tree just outside the back door which provided a giant sculpture for roses to ramble over, to the beautifully tended flowerbeds, full of a fascinating mix of Victorian and Edwardian flowers spelling the mystery and magic of a more tranquil bygone age. And Essie just loved it.

As she opened the gnarled oak door, her gaze roamed over the polished wood floor and deep raspberry-sherbert sofa and chairs, the richness of the colours enhanced by the glow of the dying sunlight, and—as always—the peace and joy her home brought her flooded her heart with thankfulness. This was hers— all hers. Never mind that she would probably be paying for it for the rest of her working life—it was *hers*.

And whatever it took to keep her home— even if she had to travel for hours each day, if a new job meant she'd be in a different district—she'd do it gladly. Here, she was her own mistress and answerable to no one; here, she felt safe and secure and impregnable.

The sudden ringing of the telephone interrupted her reverie and brought her back to the real world with a jolt. Not another panic at the practice? She groaned out loud before lifting the receiver. The last thing she needed tonight was a home visit somewhere. May was technically Jamie's month for being available, but if he was already out on another call and the case was urgent, then Peter would ring her. And if they were both out her boss—very reluctantly—would turn out, too.

'Esther Russell.' The clipped intonation had never put Peter off from ordering her out in the past, but Essie lived in hope. 'Can I help you?'

'So you do use your proper name, on occasion?' The deep, husky voice made her heart stop beating and then, as Xavier said, 'It suits you so much better than Essie,' her heart started racing at twice its normal rate.

'Who is this?' She knew exactly who it was, but she wasn't going to give him the satisfaction of knowing that.

'Xavier.' It was very dry.

'Oh.' Essie's throat constricted and she had to swallow twice before she could say, 'How did you get my number?'

'I didn't think it was a secret?'

'No, of course it's not, but...' Her voice trailed away and she took a deep breath. 'I thought we'd said all that could be said this afternoon.' It came out brisk and steady and she was proud of herself.

'Really? That's strange, because I didn't think we said anything of note this afternoon,' Xavier said with silky emphasis.

She loathed this man. One hundred per cent, no-holds-barred, complete and utter loathing...

There was a lengthy silence, and, averse as Essie was to be the first to break it, she found herself saying, 'What do you want?'

If he answered that honestly, she'd slam the phone down on him, for sure. Xavier permitted himself a wry smile but his voice betrayed no amusement as he said, 'I don't want anything, Essie.'

And pigs fly.

This time, she was determined not to speak. After some thirty seconds had crept by with crippling slowness, Xavier said, his voice cool and remote, 'You don't believe me?'

'No, I don't,' she snapped hotly.

'Why?'

'Because the male sex always has a hidden agenda.' It was out before she could call it back and she could have kicked herself at the slip. It was dangerous to reveal anything of herself to this man, and that last sentence had divulged far, far too much. Her mouth trembled and she bit hard on her bottom lip, using the pain and the salty taste of blood to steady her resolve before she continued, her voice firm, 'Look, Xavier, I've just got in and I need a shower and something to eat, so if you've nothing specific to say…?'

'Would it make any difference if I had?' His voice was cold now and more than a little astringent.

'No.'

'Fine.'

And the phone went dead.

CHAPTER FOUR

THE violet-tinged dusk smelt of woodsmoke and roses and the rich warmth of the dying day as Essie stepped out into the garden after her shower, tugging the belt of her thick towelling robe round her waist with an irritable frown.

She normally loved this part of the day—the mellow darkness as nature settled down for the night, the odd call of the resident blackbird or thrush in the trees surrounding the lawn, and the feeling that all work was done for at least a few hours. But tonight—tonight she was all at sixes and sevens, she thought fretfully. And it was *his* fault. Nothing had been the same since she had met him.

She wandered across to the ancient wooden bench set under an old lilac tree and plumped down onto the wood, shutting her eyes with a deep sigh. Everything was going wrong, suddenly. Just over a week ago, she had had a job she adored with a passion, a home she loved to distraction, and had thought her future was set out before her like a calm, tranquil sea. And then she had met Xavier Grey and suddenly she was in the middle of a storm that threatened everything. And she had fought so hard for what she had now.

She leant back against the sun-warmed wood as she let her mind wander in a way she rarely did these days.

She had been just ten years old when her father had been killed in a car crash and twelve when her mother had married Colin Fulton. The next few years, until she had finally escaped to university, had been hell on earth.

Colin had been a widower. He had brought his three children with him when he had moved in with her mother, and at first she had thought everything was going to be wonderful. But within days of the marriage ceremony the kind, attentive father-figure who had courted her mother for six months had turned into a harsh authoritarian despot who had thought nothing of using his fists to implement his rigid, tyrannical regime. She had realised then why his natural children were so quiet and withdrawn, never speaking unless they were spoken to and behaving like three small shadows instead of normal youngsters.

But she had rebelled. Essie's eyes darkened as the long-ago sounds of repeated beatings filled the shadowed garden. She had fought him every inch of the way and if it hadn't been for her fear of leaving her mother alone with him she would have left the house long before she did. But her mother had died just one month after Essie had sat her A levels, and although the death certificate had stated a heart attack, Essie would always believe Colin had killed her mother with his cruelty. It had been after her mother's death—actually at her funeral—that she had discovered from one of his former wife's friends that the first Mrs Fulton had committed suicide. And she could understand why.

But her mother's death had freed her. She had left the family home within twenty-four hours and she had never gone back or contacted her stepfather by letter or phone.

Her stepbrother—the oldest of Colin's three children—had written to her just after she had gone to veterinary college from university when he had first left home, and they had subsequently met a few times and now kept in touch occasionally. He, like her, loathed Colin, but her stepfather's two daughters were still living at home and, according to their brother, were never likely to leave. Their father had broken their spirit early on and they were merely two living puppets under his absolute control.

Essie shook herself, a sudden shiver shooting down her spine in spite of the warmth of the evening. What an existence those girls were going to endure—and that had been the thought that had stayed with her since the moment she had left the family home, all those years before.

She shifted on the bench, her eyes watching a big, fat velvet bumble-bee in its lazy sojourn amongst the flowers as her mind wandered on. You had to live with a violent, cruel man to truly understand the horror of it, she thought bitterly. The constant gnawing fear, the degradation, the inner fight not to give in to his demands to subjugate and control and enslave, even the shame of being relieved when he was venting his wrath on someone else because it meant you were not the focus for a little while.

She had gone to university an emotional mess and, when she had met Andrew in the first week, he had been kind and gentle and seemingly besotted by her. She had fallen for him hook, line and sinker. And he had used her; oh, boy, had he used her...

She rose abruptly, walking across to the climbing white roses that scaled the old stone wall to one side of the ancient potting shed, and breathed in their sweet, heavy fragrance, her eyes shutting. But she couldn't shut out the memories tonight; for some reason they were determined to have free rein.

She hadn't realised he had seen her as nothing more than a trophy—'the most beautiful girl in the university', was how he'd put it, one night—until one of her friends, who was seeing one of Andrew's friends, had come to her, not able to bear watching her being taken for a ride any longer.

Apparently, Andrew had had a string of one-night stands all the time he was supposedly devoted just to her, and she—gullible fool that she'd been—had been doing his washing and ironing, cooking his meals, giving him money when he needed it... She had just been so overwhelmed, so thrilled to have found someone who loved her, that nothing had seemed too much for this wonderful being. How could she have been so *stupid*?

The familiar bitter frustration and deep caustic humiliation that always accompanied thoughts of Andrew snapped her eyes open.

She had been working every hour of the day and night to pay for her education, studying desperately to get the necessary grades and running round after Andrew the rest of the time—no wonder when she had finished with him she had nearly had a nervous breakdown.

But she had come out of the hurt and anguish stronger. She looked across at the house and nodded silently to herself. Much stronger. It had taken a long time but she'd done it, and now she knew exactly what she wanted out of life and it certainly didn't include a man. Her career and her home were all that mattered.

At the moment the beautiful little cottage was sparsely furnished—just a stove in the kitchen, a second-hand two- seater suite in the sitting room that she'd made new covers for and a bed upstairs, but she'd get the other things—a fridge, washing machine, microwave, TV, dresser, wardrobe and so on—as her finances allowed. She didn't care how long it took, because she was her own boss. She had all the time in the world.

And Xavier Grey? The thought came from nowhere and she spun away from the roses, her mouth hardening. He was nothing, no one; he didn't count. She would never let any man count again.

'Peter, you can't do this. You can't. Please, please reconsider.'

'Okay, Essie, so you tell me the alternatives, eh? Has Jamie got even the sniff of another job? Have you? And if I accept McFarlane's offer he'll bring his two sons and that'll be that. This way, you and Jamie get to keep your jobs, your homes, everything—nothing will change.'

Nothing would change? Was he mad? Essie stared at her boss, who was clearly more than a little irritated by her reaction to the news he considered great. Xavier Grey had put in an offer—an excellent offer, Peter had emphasised—for the house and practice and was more than agreeable to Essie and Jamie staying on and keeping the surgery a working practice, while he used the flat as an apartment for when he was in England. Apparently, he had business connections in both Dorking and Crawley and considered the practice just far enough away from the towns to be relaxing and near enough to be convenient.

'But Xavier Grey is not a *vet*.' Her voice was too shrill and she tried to moderate it as she continued, 'Why on earth would he want to take on a veterinary practice, Peter? He could get a flat or an apartment anywhere, for goodness' sake! This is just crazy.'

Peter Hargreaves looked at the slender young woman in front of him, whom he had always considered quite breathtakingly lovely, and now his voice was dry when he said, 'Why don't you ask him? He was going to ring you the other night, when we first discussed the possibility of him being interested in the property, but he didn't, then?'

Essie stared back into the bland face of her boss, her cheeks flushing as she remembered that phone call. 'He did ring but...but I was busy,' she said uncomfortably. Peter said nothing. 'And I will call him,' she added militantly. 'I don't understand any of this.'

'Okay, Essie.' Peter knew a little of her history—she had opened up to Carol one night, with the bare outline of her life before coming to the practice, and the two of them had had the intuition to fill in most of what Essie hadn't said—and now his knowledge made his voice soft when he added, 'But just remember this is Jamie's job we're talking about, too. All right? Here's Xavier's number; ring him from here if you like.'

This wasn't fair. Her eyes spoke it but she didn't give him a verbal answer before she turned and marched out of the practice's little office. And she would ring Xavier from the privacy of her own home later. She didn't want an audience for what she might say to him!

As it was, she didn't have to telephone him, because the man himself was on the doorstep within a couple of hours of her conversation with Peter.

It was a beautiful morning and May had just turned into June in style, the brilliant blue sky overhead flecked with white clouds, causing the birds to sing as they swooped and soared high overhead in the thermals, glad to be alive. But Essie wasn't thinking of the weather as she met Xavier in the hall, when she'd just finished surgery and Xavier had just arrived. In fact, she wasn't thinking of anything at all—the shock of seeing him so unexpectedly had caused her brain to go numb.

And then it started working again with a vengeance and in quite the wrong way. It told her first of all he looked incredible—hard and handsome and disturbingly like the hero of one of those spaghetti westerns, all ruthless magnificence and dark, cool control. And then it further compounded the treachery by adding that she had been seeing him in her mind's eye constantly over the past days and nights, and when she hadn't been fighting seeing him— when she'd been asleep or involved in an intricate case or something—he had been there still, on the perimeter of her consciousness, affecting everything she did.

'Good morning,' said Xavier softly.

Peter, who had answered the door and was already on the first foot of the stairs, displayed unusual tact as he chimed in, 'Come up when you're ready, Xavier. You know the way by now.'

Xavier saw her eyes narrow and it was clear she wasn't exactly over the moon at his presence, but her voice was clear and steady when she said, 'Good morning. Peter didn't say you were coming today.'

'He didn't know. I didn't know myself until a short while ago.'

'He—Peter—told me you want to buy the practice?'

It wasn't at all how she had planned to speak to him; she'd intended to ring in the quiet privacy of her small sitting room after a fortifying gin and tonic and be cool and controlled, but now her voice was threatening to betray her agitation and she forced it back into the even tone she had used seconds before as she added, 'Is that right?'

'Yes.' It was immediate.

'Why?'

'Many reasons.'

Essie stared at him. Of course he had the right to buy anything he liked—she knew that, she told herself firmly, and it was nothing to do with her. She had no right to ask him anything about his motives, not really. She wouldn't blame him if he told her to mind her own business. The last thought did more to moderate her tone than anything else as she said, 'Could you tell me a few of them?'

'Are you interested?' It was cool and laconic and told her he was thoroughly enjoying having her at such a disadvantage. But then, that shouldn't have surprised her—all men were the same under the skin. Some of them just had better skins than others, that was all, and she had to admit—much as she hated to—that Xavier Grey's was something special in that it covered a prize-winning frame.

'Of course.' It was a tight snap and she could have kicked herself for letting him see he'd caught her on the raw. That was definitely not the way to handle this. 'I work here, don't I?' she added more primly.

He folded his arms across a chest broad enough to get lost in and her heartbeat went crazy. His arms were tanned and muscular and, like last time, he was wearing a denim shirt and jeans but this time they were black and enhanced the impression of brooding masculinity tenfold. He was lethal. She eyed him uneasily.

'Yes, you work here, Essie,' he said silkily, the piercing silver-blue eyes roaming over her heart-shaped face for some moments before he added, 'But that doesn't mean I have to tell you my reasons for a private transaction with your boss, does it?'

'No,' she admitted reluctantly, 'but if you're not ashamed of them I think it's a perfectly reasonable request, in the circumstances.'

Reasonable didn't come into this. Xavier's expression was unreadable and he kept it that way when he said, 'Maybe, maybe not, but such matters are not for discussion in the middle of a busy working morning, I presume. I'll talk to you later if you insist. Over dinner?'

He was making it sound as if she was forcing him to have dinner with her! Essie stared at him, speechless, and then she managed a somewhat weak, 'I'm on late afternoon surgery tonight and then I'm on call.'

'What time will you finish here?'

'Some time after seven, probably half-past.'

'Fine.' He smiled but it was definitely a crocodile smile. 'I'll be here for seven and we'll take it from there.'

'But what about lunchtime? I could spare half an hour then—'

'Sorry.' He cut into her babbling in a clipped tone that made it clear he didn't consider she was doing him any favours. 'I'm busy until later.'

Oh, hell. This was clearly going to be on his terms or not at all.

'I'd have to go home and change,' Essie prevaricated lamely.

'No problem.'

The lazy drawl was back; he'd got what he wanted and he was all charm now, Essie thought savagely, and she *hated* him!

'I could keep you waiting for ages,' she warned him stiffly.

He looked straight into her stormy blue eyes and there was a definite glint in his when he said, 'No, you won't, Essie. Trust me.'

Huh, so he thought he could control the whole animal kingdom as well, did he? Essie thought acidly. She wanted to say something really cold and cutting but her mind was blank, and all she managed was a fairly tight, 'Well, don't say I didn't warn you I'm on call.'

'I'll remember you warned me, Essie.' He knew he shouldn't do this—she was as skittish as a young colt and twice as temperamental—but the desire to kiss her was stronger than the cautionary voice in his head, and he reached out a careful hand and cupped the side of her face in surprisingly gentle fingers as he tilted her head to meet his onslaught.

Her lips were tightly closed against his mouth but, as they touched, he felt the tremble she couldn't hide and it filled him with elation. She might not like him—she *definitely* didn't like him—but there was a powerful sexual attraction between them that was mind-blowing, and she felt it every bit as much as he did.

'*Don't.*' Essie jerked away but it was too late; the rush of heat that had exploded at his touch was plain to see and Xavier was looking.

'You want me, Essie.' His voice was low and rough and his eyes were brilliant in the muted light of the hall, his big body all clothed in black frightening her even as it thrilled something deep inside. 'Your body knows me, even if your mind is determined to make us adversaries.'

'No.' She took a step backwards, her voice wild. 'You stay away from me.'

'You want me,' he said again in answer, the strangely beautiful eyes sweeping over her body in a way that made her aware of the taut peaks of her breasts beneath the thin T-shirt she was wearing. In spite of herself, she crossed her arms over her chest, her eyes enormous as they stared back into the mesmerising gaze.

'I don't.' Her voice was stronger now but the trembling was worse and she felt crushed at how easily he had mastered her senses. The feeling reminded her of Andrew's subtle domination and of her stepfather's cruel brute

force, and everything in Essie rebelled as a
hundred and one ignominious memories joined
together into one massive mortifying whole.
'You men are all the same, aren't you?' she
bit out wildly. 'You're only ever interested in
one thing.'

'Essie—'

Something in her face had shocked him but
she didn't give him a chance to continue as
she swung away from him towards the back of
the house on winged feet, fairly flying across
the large square hall without a backward
glance and pulling open the heavy fire door
that led into the area where the well-equipped
operating room and animal quarters were.

She heard him call her name once but he
didn't follow her into the rear of the property.
As she dived into the recovery room adjacent
to the small operating theatre, all was quiet
antiseptic and sterile formality.

She stayed in the white-walled room for
some minutes; as her heartbeat slowed and reason returned, an awful sense of embarrassment
had her groaning out loud. What must he think
of her? He had only kissed her—if the brief
caress could be called even that—and she had

reacted like a scalded cat. He'd think she was deranged, or worse.

The big tomcat she had operated on that morning—he'd been involved in a ferocious fight with another feline and had come off the worst—was watching her with wide, unblinking green eyes. When her tortured gaze could focus on something other than the horror of how she'd behaved, she noticed him and squatted down by the slatted cage, her voice soft as she said, 'Oh, Winston, if only everything was as simple for me as it is for you.'

The emerald eyes reproached her —Winston considered defending his patch from the countless assaults attempted by the neighbouring hoods intent on a coup more than enough problems for any self-respecting cat—but as Essie opened the cage and checked his stitches, fussing him as she did so, he purred and capitulated. She didn't understand—you couldn't expect these humans to appreciate the finer points of guerrilla warfare—but she was warm and kind and she had gentle hands and a sad voice and he liked her.

Essie stayed for some time, stroking the big tomcat until he was fast asleep again, and then she checked the other two occupied cages before making her way to the surgery kitchen at the very back of the house, where she made herself a very strong coffee which she drank scalding hot. This was going to be a long and busy day and that was quite enough to cope with at the moment—she'd think about the evening when she had to.

As fate would have it—and Essie was beginning to suspect Xavier controlled that, too— she finished evening surgery early and was ready to leave the practice by seven o'clock— an almost unheard-of occurrence. There had been none of the usual last-minute appointments, no panics, no accidents—just nice normal patients who slotted neatly into their allotted schedule.

And as though he knew—which he couldn't, he just couldn't, Essie reassured herself silently as she shut the door on the last client— Xavier had arrived early at ten to seven, joining the last remaining patient, a massive Dobermann and his master, in the waiting room.

She hadn't expected to see him there and, when she had popped her head round the door to usher her patient through, it had been a nasty moment. Xavier had been sitting, one leg crossed casually over the other knee and his arms spread out on top of the long bench-like seat, making easy conversation with the Dobermann's owner, and he had looked up as she had entered. And then he'd smiled. Which wasn't anything in itself, *nothing*—a smile was a smile was a smile—but the difference it had made to the hard, masculine face had taken her breath away.

But she'd handled the situation perfectly well, she told herself now as she walked back into the waiting room—she'd been cool, calm and capable, as befitted her position.

'Do you deal with many great brutes like that?'

'What?' Xavier had risen at her entrance and now the sight of him, clad in charcoal trousers and a dark peacock-blue silk shirt and tie as he towered over her, was somewhat over-whelming, and she had to readjust her thought processes before she could say, 'What do you mean?'

'The Hound of the Baskervilles.' He indi-cated the hall with a flick of his head. 'I wouldn't like to get too near those jaws, my-self.'

Essie looked hard at him to see if he was being patronising but she saw to her surprise he was perfectly genuine. It suddenly felt wonderfully good to know she had impressed him. It enabled her to say, her voice light, 'Oh, Cuthbert is as gentle as a kitten. Most of the big dogs are; it's the small ones who are more likely to give you a nasty nip if you aren't careful.'

'Do you get bitten often?'

'Occasionally, but you sort of develop a sixth sense about the ones that might react that way. Most animals are fine if you know how to handle them.'

This was the first time he had got her talking, really talking, and Xavier was surprised how important it was to him. As surprised as he'd been when he'd found himself discussing that offer with Peter Hargreaves, he reminded himself silently. But then this whole affair was crazy and he'd lost count of how many times he'd told himself he was nuts to take it any further.

'I'd like to see where you work—the operating room and so on.' He kept his voice very casual. 'Peter was going to show me some time—but if you've a minute or two to spare now?'

There was a moment of silence when he was aware of her searching eyes and then she said, her voice uncertain, 'You really want to see?'

'Please.'

'Why?'

Because all this means so much to you and I want to understand why; I want to *see* for myself. 'I'm just curious, that's all,' he said nonchalantly. 'But if you'd rather not...'

This time the silence was longer and then Essie said, her voice low, 'No, I'll show you, if you're really interested.'

'Thank you,' Xavier said quietly, his eyes holding hers until she broke the contact by turning abruptly away.

She shouldn't have agreed to show him around. The thought was immediate and accompanied a hot panic that made her skin tingle. She should have told him he'd have to do that with Peter and made it clear she was seeing him purely on sufferance tonight. There could be no meeting-point between them, not with the sort of man he was. Oh, she was a fool; she was a twenty-four-carat fool.

Surprisingly, the little tour went amazingly well. Within a couple of minutes, Essie found herself relaxing enough to answer Xavier's clear, well-informed questions and comments quite naturally and, as always when talking about the work she loved with such passion, her face became animated and her eyes sparkled.

It was when they re-emerged into the front part of the house, Xavier's car being parked in the drive outside, that Essie realised the last fifteen minutes or so had probably been a very clever strategy on his part. And again she reminded herself she was a gullible fool and that she couldn't afford to be, not around Xavier Grey.

She watched him as he opened the front door for her, standing aside and allowing her to precede him into the warm, mellow evening air. He was a smoothie. He was, he was a real smoothie when he wanted to be, in spite of the cold, rugged outer shell and almost frightening remoteness that seemed habitual.

'What's the matter?'

He had reached her side and was looking down at her, and now she blinked a little at the frown on his face.

'The matter?' Everything, absolutely everything, and the worst of it is I've promised to
have dinner with you. 'Nothing; I'm just a bit
tired, that's all. It's been an exhausting day.'
She forced a smile. 'Look, if you'd rather meet
me somewhere later, that's fine by me,' she
said quickly, before she lost her nerve. She
didn't want him in her home. *She did not want
this man in her home.* 'I've got to have a bath
and change and get ready, and I'm quite happy
to drive myself and meet you somewhere if
you want to relax with a drink. I can't drink if
I'm on call and it's silly for both of us to ab-
stain,' she finished brightly. 'And I really need
my own transport, anyway.'

He looked down at her, his gaze implacable.
'I thought of all that earlier,' he said quietly.

'You did?' He had taken her arm and ushered her over to his car and now her gaze focused on the back seat. There were a couple
of large cardboard boxes there filled with all
manner of groceries; she could see steaks,
salad, wine...

'I'm going to cook for you while you have
a bath and get changed,' he said easily, 'and
then you can have a good meal and a glass of

wine in the comfort of your own home. One glass won't hurt,' he added softly.

Essie thought of her tiny kitchen and blinked. And then she thought of Xavier Grey downstairs while she bathed, of him perched at the minuscule breakfast bar that separated the kitchen area from the sitting room and served as a dining-room table, and she blinked again. She'd been given two old bar-stools for the breakfast bar but she hadn't got round to covering them in the same material as the sofa and chairs yet, and they were distinctly shabby.

'There's no need for you to cook for me,' she said hastily—too hastily. 'Peter can contact me on my mobile if there's a call and—'

'I insist.'

Essie swallowed dryly.

'And stop being afraid of me,' he said evenly.

'What?' Her back straightened and her chin jutted out as though someone had pressed a button. 'I'm not afraid of you. Don't be so ridiculous,' she said with icy disdain. 'It's just that the kitchen is tiny and I've hardly got anything—'

'Have you got a grill and a couple of plates and glasses?' he interrupted her coolly.

'Yes, but—'

'Then you don't need anything else.'

What she *needed* was the reassuring anonymity of a restaurant populated with other people, Essie thought wryly. A cosy twosome in her little nest was definitely unthinkable.

But, unthinkable or not, Xavier just ignored her continued protests and somehow she found herself installed in the front seat of the beautiful Mercedes before she could blink.

She watched Xavier as he walked round the bonnet of the gleaming car and slid easily into the driving seat and her stomach contracted at his closeness. He smelt good, wonderful, and he looked so…so… Her mind refused to come up with an adequate description and stuttered to a halt.

'Directions?' He turned to her, his eyes warning her not to prevaricate any further.

'Oh, yes, of course.' She had jumped at the sound of his voice and she hoped he hadn't noticed the slight involuntary movement which spoke of her taut nerves. She gave him brief instructions, adding, 'It's just a couple of minutes in the car but the last mile or so is a bit winding.'

'No problem.'

There *was* a problem—a huge, massive, *gigantic* problem—and it was sitting right next to her. Essie sat stiff and silent, her hands gripped tightly together on her lap as she stared straight ahead with rigid control. This was crazy. How had she ever got in this mess anyway? she asked herself tensely. And surely he couldn't be serious about buying Peter's house and keeping the surgery running? It was all so…surreal.

There he sat, in his designer clothes and his Rolex watch, driving his darn great Mercedes, and he was seriously asking her to believe he was interested in an insignificant little veterinary practice? He wouldn't really spend thousands of pounds just to bring her to heel, would he? So he could have control of her employment, her working life? No one could take a grudge that far…could they? And she'd bet he didn't even like animals.

'Do you like animals?' It was out before she had time to consider her words.

She expected some reaction after she'd spoken—surprise, a quick glance her way—but he merely pondered her words in the cool, imperturbable way he had, and then said quietly, 'Yes, I do, although I have to say I've had little contact with any. My upbringing wasn't conducive to having pets.'

'Why?' She turned fully to the cold, hard profile.

'There wasn't enough food to fill our stomachs, let alone those of any cats or dogs,' he said shortly.

It was the last thing she had expected him to say and, for a moment, she just stared at him. 'I'm sorry,' she said at last. 'I didn't mean to pry.'

'I know that.' They were almost home—the Mercedes had covered the short distance with consummate ease—but now Xavier pulled into the side of the road and switched off the engine before turning to her, his face expressionless and his voice steady as he said, 'I need to explain something to you before we go any further, Essie. You seem to have got the idea I come from a wealthy background, that I've had a privileged upbringing—'

'No, not exactly. I mean, Janice said you'd made your own fortune,' she interrupted quickly.

'Whatever your home is like, it will be a palace compared to the hovel I was raised in,' Xavier continued quietly, as though she hadn't spoken. 'When my mother left England, she was pregnant with her first child, my half-sister, Natalie, and the circumstances were painful.' He paused a moment. 'Within eighteen months of Natalie being born, the man my mother had run away with—who was not her husband—had left her, and she had no money and no friends: an alien in a strange land.'

His eyes had left hers to look out of the car window, but Essie could still see that talking like this was difficult for him. He didn't open up like this normally, she thought with a bolt of intuition. This was unfamiliar territory for him.

'My mother wasn't unkind to us—not physically, anyway—but she was promiscuous,' he said heavily. 'By the time she was expecting me she didn't know who the father was and the next few years were ones of drinking and wild parties, by all accounts. I don't remember too much, but Natalie was several years older than me and she bore the brunt of it, and brought me up, too. My mother was rarely around and when she was she wasn't sober.

And then, when Natalie was fourteen, one of the men my mother had brought home—' He stopped abruptly, turning from her and drawing in a deep breath as a muscle clenched in his square jaw.

'Oh, no.' Essie's heart was thudding. How awful, how terrible.

'The outcome of the rape was Candy and Natalie was barely fifteen when she died giving birth to her. The shock of it all and the guilt she felt surprisingly had the effect of putting my mother on the wagon, but she'd damaged her body to the point where she was never well. But she looked after Candy until she was too ill to do so any more, and by that time I was eighteen and making enough money to keep us.'

'I'm so sorry, Xavier.' She didn't know what else to say but her soft whisper brought his eyes focusing on her face again with something like surprise in their silver depths.

He shrugged abruptly, clearly disturbed he had said so much. 'It doesn't matter; it's all in the past,' he said crisply. 'But I wanted you to know I wasn't born with a silver spoon in my mouth and I appreciate hard graft when I see it. You're prepared to work for what you want and so is that other guy… Jack, is it?'

'Jamie,' Essie corrected quickly.

'Right, Jamie. I had a long chat with him the last time I was here, and I liked him.'

Jamie hadn't said. Essie felt a pang of hurt before common sense cut in and said silently, Well, he wouldn't, would he, knowing how you feel about Xavier? Least said, soonest mended, would be Jamie's motto. Anything for a trouble-free life.

'So…' Xavier's voice was brisk. 'Do you feel better about my taking you home?'

Better? She felt a thousand times worse, Essie thought helplessly. She didn't want to know that his childhood had been so awful, that he had loved his sister so deeply and now cared for her offspring as though Candy were his own daughter. No wonder Candy loved him so much—it was because he had been everything to her: mother, father, friend, confidante, Essie acknowledged reluctantly.

But Candy was Candy and how he felt about his niece was not how he felt about her, she reminded herself sharply in the next instant. She just didn't believe that his motives for buying Peter's property were purely philanthropic; it didn't fit the facts of what she knew about this hard-bitten business mogul with the love-'em-and-leave-'em mentality Janice had told her about.

'Essie?'

He was asking her if she felt better about the evening ahead and, after all he had revealed, she had to lie, and convincingly. But she hesitated just a moment too long for the keen, astute eyes fixed on her face.

'What is it with you anyway?' he asked roughly a millisecond later, before she could respond. 'Don't you ever give an inch with anyone?'

'Do you?' she bit back immediately, stung at his tone.

Xavier drew in a deep breath and exhaled slowly before he said, his voice wry now, 'No, I guess I don't, at that, but aren't women supposed to be the softer sex?'

'Softer, as in credulous?' Her voice was cold now and accusatory.

Xavier settled back in his seat, raking back a lock of jet-black hair as the silver gaze took in the fiery colour staining her high cheekbones. 'Who was he, Essie?' he asked softly. 'Who was the jerk who broke your heart?'

Her hands curled into fists of impotent pain and she buried them deep into the pockets of her work-worn jeans away from the piercing gaze. 'He's not important, not now,' she said tightly, her voice clipped and raw. 'And who are you to talk, anyway? I've heard you've broken a few hearts in your time.'

'Is that right?'

'Yes, yes, it's right,' Essie said fiercely, 'and I don't know why you're here now, but if you think you're going to blackmail me into sleeping with you, by holding my job like the sword of Damocles over my head—'

'That's enough.' It was grim and quiet, but his eyes positively simmered with white heat.

For a moment she was scared, *petrified*, transported back to the days when she was a child and such a tone was the prelude to being used as Colin's punchbag, but then she forced herself to speak. 'Don't you dare hit me,' she said. 'Don't you dare.'

'Hit you?' She had metamorphosed in front of his eyes; she was all woman and yet there was someone else behind her eyes, someone small and terrified who nevertheless was fighting back. And it stunned him. It quite literally stunned him. 'For crying out loud, Essie, I wasn't going to hit you.' He swore softly at the fear in her face. 'I've no time for any man who would raise his hand to a woman, whatever the provocation,' he said gently. 'Believe me. I'm not going to hurt you; I would never hurt you.'

She was as stiff as a board, her eyes enormous as she stared into his face.

'Is that what he did, Essie? He hit you?' Xavier couldn't believe how fiercely he wanted to kill someone he didn't know. 'Not all men are like that, sweetheart.'

It was the gentleness in the last words that did it. Rage she could cope with—disappointment, hurt or mockery, even—but the tenderness in the big dark man in front of her was too much and she howled. She just howled.

The tears came from her eyes, her nose, her mouth in an unflattering flood that she could do nothing about, and even when he pulled her close, gathering her into him in a tight embrace as he murmured soothing words of comfort above her head, she couldn't move. She didn't want to move…

CHAPTER FIVE

XAVIER found he had his own set of problems as he cradled Essie's soft, yielding body against his.

One, the last thing he needed in all the world—the very last thing—was any kind of emotional involvement with a woman.

Two, he especially didn't need any emotional involvement with this one. She had got under his skin in a way he didn't like, and he found himself wishing he had done what his instinct had been telling him to do since the first time he had set eyes on her, and hightailed it away as soon as he could.

Three, she didn't like him or trust him, and he was damned if he was going to beg or plead to alter the status quo.

Four, she clearly had enough baggage from the past to need someone a damn sight more committed than him.

Five, he was supposed to be comforting her right now, when what he really wanted to do was something much less noble, and although his brain was telling him to back off his body was away on a jaunt of its own.

He was as hard as a rock, and unless she was as innocent as a newborn babe she was going to cotton on very soon. It was the scent of her, the feel of her—her warmth, her feminine fragrance that was a mix of a faint flowery perfume and a bodily heat that was purely her own. Hell, he hadn't wanted a woman like this for a long, long time...

Essie wasn't as innocent as a newborn babe.

Although she had never allowed Andrew full intimacy, she had thought she was in love with him and would be with him for the rest of her life, and their skirmishes—which had always come about by Andrew trying to push the boundaries she had laid down just a little further—had acquainted her with the feel of a fully aroused male.

That she hadn't been equally aroused or even really interested in any sort of intimacy with Andrew she had put down to a lack of something in herself.

It wasn't until a good few months after she had finished with Andrew and was coming out of the morass of despair and bitter pain that she'd realised she had actually disliked his wet-mouthed kisses and general indifference to her feelings, his lack of finesse when he caressed her and his obsession with her giving in to his sugar-coated demands.

She had decided then that Andrew must have been right—she was frigid. He had told her she was, often enough—listing girls who were sleeping around each time he did so. She had been too naive to realise at the time he was speaking from first-hand knowledge! But now, as she leant against Xavier's hard frame, the warmth and hunger heating her skin told her she was far from frigid. But then she'd known that the first time he had touched her. And she'd known he wanted her, too, as his body was now more than adequately demonstrating.

'I'm…I'm all right.' She spoke the words on a little hiccup as she moved back into her own seat and he didn't try to stop her. But it was too late. She could still feel the sensation of her body locked into his, the way they had fitted like a warm living jigsaw, the male smell and feel of him. No wonder he only had to lift his little finger and the women flocked round if he could make them feel like this with such little effort, she thought ruefully.

'Do you want to talk about it?'

'What?' For an awful moment she thought he was referring to her lusting after his body, but then she took hold of herself, accepting the big white handkerchief he held out to her with a bob of her head and dabbing frantically at her face, before saying, 'No, not really. It's...it's old history.'

It wasn't so old if she could still cry like that. Xavier surveyed her with silver-blue eyes that hid his thoughts. She still had some personal demons to face, if he knew anything about it—and he knew all about personal demons, all right.

He nodded slowly. 'Think about talking to someone some time, Essie,' he said in an easy drawl. 'Not me—someone you trust, okay? It helps.'

She eyed him uncertainly.

'Okay?' he repeated softly.

'Okay.' She sniffed and rubbed at her nose again. She must look a mess. She hadn't looked too good before the wailing and moaning, she reflected miserably as Xavier started the engine again, but now...

She watched him stretch his big body and settle himself into the seat more comfortably before he eased the car into the mild flow of traffic the small Sussex town boasted, and again her nerves twanged as her body reacted to the overt maleness. He was dangerous, and he was the last person on earth she would think of getting involved with—but oh, boy, he was dynamite, she thought with a hunger that actually shocked her and had the effect of a dousing of cold water.

'Turn left down here.' It was only a few hundred yards from where they had been parked, but as Essie directed him down a narrow country lane towards the cottage the vista changed dramatically.

The lane had the odd cottage at the top of it, properties that were six or seven times as big as Essie's and set well back from the road, with beautifully laid-out front gardens making floral tunnels in the warmth and sunshine of south- facing slopes, but within a moment or two there were just fields on either side of the country lane.

The Mercedes ate up the half a mile or so before Essie's home came into view, its white-painted exterior glowing in the late evening sunshine. 'That's it.' Essie pointed to the tiny house and the small pull-in at the fore of the

front garden. 'You can park there.' She indicated the space beside her faithful old Escort.

'This is your cottage?'

She couldn't gauge anything from his face
or voice, and her own was slightly rueful as
she said, 'To be strictly truthful, it's the building society's.'

She clambered out of the car before he could
open her door for her and waited for him to
join her by the rickety front gate, her gaze intent as she watched him look around before
slowly walking to her side.

A warm summer breeze was ruffling the
tops of the trees surrounding the cottage, and
the evening resounded with the faint sound of
church bells somewhere in the distance as bell-
ringers practised their craft. Xavier turned to
her, and again she could read nothing in his
face. 'This is just beautiful,' he said softly. 'I
can see you living here.'

'Can you?'

Essie didn't stop to contemplate exactly
what he meant; she opened the gate and
walked swiftly up the narrow winding path to
the front door, her heart thudding. She was
having some sort of brainstorm; it was the only
explanation, she told herself feverishly. How

else did you explain her delight at seeing him here? She'd already decided earlier that she didn't want him within a mile of her or her home, and nothing, *nothing* had changed.

'How long have you lived here?'

He had joined her at the front door and she trembled at his closeness as she fumbled with her key.

'Just over eighteen months,' she said tightly, her relief as the door swung open overwhelming. 'It needed completely renovating inside, so I was living here with a sleeping bag and a camping stove for a while, and I've hardly got any furniture yet, but that will come with time. The property and where it is were the main things.'

He followed her inside, glancing round the whitewashed walls and beamed ceiling, and then he turned his head, his eyes locking with hers as he said, his voice gruff, 'You're quite a lady.'

'Not really.' She was beginning to babble and she knew it. 'I just wanted somewhere away from the madding crowd, you know? And this was so small and in such awful condition, most people weren't interested—'

He bent his head and took her lips with his own and time stopped. She didn't want to respond—she knew it was utter folly—but the kiss was timeless and enchanting and everything Andrew's assaults had never been.

There was a fire inside her that was beginning to burn, dangerously feeding the need that was overpowering and terribly potent. The taste, the essence of him spun in her head, filling the quintessence of her mind, and his mouth was urgent and hungry and indescribably sensual.

If he started to really make love to her she wouldn't be able to stop him, she thought raggedly as the sweetness spread through her blood like honey. All that he'd revealed about his childhood and youth had mellowed the edges of her distrust and the sexual fantasies— which had been unknown before she had met him, but which had invaded her psyche recently at unguarded moments—consolidated in an aching need that was shattering.

Only he didn't make love to her. He raised his head, very calmly, and said, 'Right, I'll fetch the things in from the car and get started while you relax in a hot tub. Call if you need someone to scrub your back.' And then he turned and walked out into the spangled sunlight outside.

Essie drew in a deep shuddering breath and then she sighed helplessly, shutting her eyes tight for a moment before racing up the dangerously narrow staircase in a way that just begged for a broken leg.

Once in her petite bedroom, which held her three-quarter-size pine bed and nothing else—her wardrobe being a makeshift bar which she had nailed to the wall, for the time being—she sank down onto the pretty coverlet and stared at the polished wood floor. She had lost her mind. She twisted painfully, hot panic trickling over her trembling limbs. How could she be considering—even *anticipating*—starting a relationship with Xavier?

Relationship? The word mocked her with its primness. Xavier wasn't after a relationship, an inner voice told her with bald brazenness. He wanted her in his bed and he was prepared to pay for the privilege. That was what this boiled down to, if she was being honest with herself—which was more than he was being with her.

He had made it very clear he wanted her and she had inadvertently added to his desire by rejecting him in the first place—he probably hadn't had that happen before. And so he had pursued her, as a hunter pursued the prey that eluded it. As luck would have it, her circumstances had played right into his hands. He'd found himself in a prime position, all things considered. He could buy the practice and no doubt get someone in to run it for him whilst he continued with his normal life, flitting down to Sussex when he felt like a quick romp in the hay.

Essie bit her lip hard. The practice was a going concern, he had a pleasant country flat for when he needed a break and he'd engineered her very much under his control—certainly as far as her bread and butter was concerned. Oh, yes, he'd got exactly what he wanted.

But he hadn't. She straightened, her mouth gathering into a tight little button. And she'd tell him he hadn't. With his wealth, the veterinary practice meant nothing to him—no doubt he could afford to buy and sell Peter ten times over and not even notice.

She didn't want to lose her job, and she didn't want Jamie to lose *his*, but she wasn't going to become Xavier Grey's mistress either.

Her heart pounded alarmingly and the rush of excitement the thought induced was even more alarming.

A bath. She needed a bath. She would wash her hair and soak away the strain of the day, and then go back downstairs to face him, refreshed and rejuvenated. And she wasn't going to dress up or put on any make-up, either—no titivating. She nodded to herself. Somehow he had inveigled his way into her home and her life but enough was enough, and the sooner he knew the score, the better it would be for both of them. If not for poor Jamie.

A delicious smell wafted towards her as Essie walked down the stairs some twenty minutes later, her hair still damp and curling about her shoulders in a riotous display of gleaming gold.

True to her earlier resolve, she was dressed simply in dark green cotton drawstring trousers and a beige sleeveless halter-necked top, her face devoid of make-up and her only adornment large golden hoops in her ears. It was too warm for shoes and her feet were bare.

She looked impossibly young and fresh, and Xavier's stomach contracted as he turned from the steaks at her approach.

'Glass of wine?' His voice was cool as he gestured at the open bottle to one side of her little mug tree. 'I didn't know what you liked so I got red and white. The red's open and the white's in a bucket of cold water outside the front door; it should be chilled enough by now.'

'The red's fine.' She flushed slightly. Everyone had a fridge, didn't they? And he was a Canadian millionaire who must be used to living the life of Riley. And then she remembered his comments on his early life and she relaxed a little. Whether he'd had a fridge or not, he knew all about struggling; she had to give him that.

The wine was just heavenly and even Essie, with her limited knowledge of such niceties, knew it must have cost a bomb. 'This tastes delicious,' she said quietly, wandering to the other side of the breakfast bar and perching on one of the threadbare stools with a natural grace that wasn't lost on the big dark man watching her with narrowed eyes.

'One of Candy's favourites,' Xavier said easily. 'She simplifies the expert's effusive description of the bouquet and so on to the description of scrumptious.' He grinned at her and her heart stopped beating.

'I don't blame her,' she managed stoutly. 'I think all that gushing is ridiculous.'

'I thought you might,' he said with a cryptic smile, turning back to the sizzling steaks.

What was it about a man cooking—especially a powerful, virile, *masculine* man like Xavier—that was so sexy? Essie asked herself feverishly. He had discarded his tie in the heat of the evening and several of his shirt buttons were undone, exposing his hard, tanned throat and the beginning of crisp body hair on his chest, and he made her legs wobbly. More than wobbly, in fact. And her breathing wasn't too good, either.

'The salad's tossed and the mushrooms and tomatoes are keeping warm in the oven,' Xavier said conversationally as she sat looking at his broad back. 'Could you find a couple of plates and knives and forks? Then I think we're just about ready.'

'Oh, yes, of course.' She was flustered and all but leapt off the stool, but then she moved

very carefully into the small space the kitchen
boasted, trying not to touch him as she reached
into the cupboard on his left. Once she had the
things on the breakfast bar, she was out of the
kitchen area like a shot.

'I don't bite, Essie.'

He was taking the steaks out from under the
grill as he spoke and for a moment she thought
she must have misheard him. 'I'm sorry?' She
stared at him as he raised his head to meet her
startled gaze.

'No, you're not.' His frown smoothed and
his expression was one of quizzical reproach.
'Do you think I'm going to leap on you? Is
that it?' he asked softly, the quietness of his
voice at odds with the intensity in his eyes.

'I'm sorry, but I don't have the faintest idea
what you're talking about,' she said stiffly.

'Two sorries, and you don't mean either of
them,' he drawled reflectively. 'You aren't at
all sorry that you're persisting in treating me
like a nasty smell, are you? In fact I think
you're more determined than ever to see me
as the enemy.'

'The enemy?' She forced a smile that was
supposed to be cool and was merely brittle.
'That's nonsense.'

He folded his arms over his chest as he studied her flushed face from under hooded lids. 'Let's eat,' he said suddenly, and he turned back to the stove, producing the mushrooms and tomatoes before reaching for the salad bowl. 'I'm starving, I don't know about you.'

She should have been starving—she should have been ravenous, because she'd hardly eaten anything all day—but with Xavier just a few inches away from her, his flagrant masculinity even more threatening for his easy unawareness of his attraction, her appetite was non-existent.

In another moment he was perched on the stool at the side of her, reaching for the wine and pouring himself another glass as he said, 'You're sticking to the one, I take it? In case your...services are needed?'

How could he make such a simple question so suggestive? Essie didn't let her thoughts show on her face as she answered him very coolly, 'Definitely. Some of the farms we look after are a good few miles away and it wouldn't be good to show up anywhere smelling of alcohol.'

'How restrained of you.'

Restrained? With his thigh brushing hers because of the ridiculously confined space, and his hard, powerful body filling her air space?

Essie gulped hard, took her knife and fork and cut into the peppered steak. It was delicious—tender and succulent and cooked to perfection—and it reminded her she hadn't thanked him either for the food or for the cooking of it.

'This is very good of you.' She smiled nervously as she darted a swift glance at the rugged male face.

'Is it?'

She met his eyes and saw the dark amusement there. He was laughing at her! The surge of annoyance swept away any nervousness and replaced it with healthy indignation, but she was determined not to rise to his bait. 'I think so.' She managed a cool smile as she turned back to her plate and speared a large, juicy mushroom.

'You get mad more quickly than any woman I've ever known.'

His voice was extremely dry and she realised she hadn't hidden her ill humour too well. 'And you've known plenty,' she fired back sweetly.

'Says who?' he asked mildly, not seeming at all put out.

'Everyone.' She made the magnificent exaggeration with a little flourish of her head.

'Everyone?' She was aware he was considering her darkly but she didn't turn her head to meet his gaze. 'Well, even if that ridiculous statement were true, I'd say it was no one's business but mine,' he drawled easily. 'I make no apology for liking the opposite sex, Essie. I've always laboured under the idea that it's what makes the world go round—attraction between men and women. The planet sure wouldn't remain inhabited for long without it.'

He had an answer for everything. Essie gritted her teeth and conceded the battle but not the war.

'Look, could we just eat the meal on a truce basis?' Xavier said a moment later. 'I for one don't want indigestion and frankly I enjoy my food, especially when I've been slaving over a hot stove for hours.'

She did glance at him then and saw the silver-blue gaze was smiling at her, the laughter lines radiating from the corners of his thickly lashed eyes very much in evidence.

She couldn't help giving a grin in response to the twinkle in his eyes, much as she didn't want to.

'That's better,' he said blandly. 'You really are far too serious, you know. All work and no play makes Jill a dull girl...'

'Thank you very much,' she returned tartly. This was the second time he had used that particular saying and it rankled badly. 'I'm sure that's something no one can accuse you of.'

'Dullness?'

'No.' She eyed him frostily. 'No play.'

'How true.'

Impossible conversation. Impossible man! Essie ate another mouthful of steak. But this meal *was* absolutely gorgeous and now her tastebuds had woken her stomach up she found she was, in fact, extremely hungry.

By the time she had cleared her plate, Xavier had risen and fetched the dessert—a mouthwatering raspberry roulade—out of its box, slicing her an enormous portion and putting it in front of her along with a carton of fresh cream. 'Tuck in.' He surveyed her warmly. 'I love a woman who eats well.'

This was too cosy by half and she had to break the spell she could feel him weaving right now. 'Xavier, about your offer—'

'Eat.' He interrupted her with a smile but there was something in his face that told her it was an order, not a suggestion. 'We'll talk over coffee.'

Essie thought about arguing but the roulade was crying out to be eaten and it was the perfect dessert after the steak and salad. She gave up, picked up her spoon and, as she dug into the wonderful concoction of cream and raspberries and sponge and all things fattening, gave a little grunt of appreciation deep in her throat. She *loved* raspberry roulade.

They polished off the roulade between them—the box said it was meant for six—although Xavier had the lion's share, as Essie was full to bursting. Once she had finished her plateful, she slid off the stool and into the kitchen, relieved to be able to put a few feet between them.

'I'll see to the coffee; why don't you go and sit down?' she suggested from the safety of the sink as she turned to look Xavier's way.

'I'll dry.' He indicated the plates she had just placed on the draining-board with an easy inclination of his head.

'No.' It was too quick and she qualified it with, 'There are only a couple of things, really, and I always let them air-dry. It's supposed to be more hygienic.' The thought of herself and Xavier squeezed into the small space was worse than the close proximity of the stools, and that had been bad enough. Her thigh was still tingling with the feel of his hard flesh next to hers.

He inclined his head again but, instead of walking across to the small suite, he wandered over to the front door, which was still open to the warm, slumberous evening, and disappeared outside.

He was obviously intending to explore the garden to the side and back of the cottage and, although it was the natural thing to do on a hot June evening when the air was still and heavy, it disturbed her. She didn't know why, but it disturbed her more than a little. It was bad enough that he had been in her home, that she would now picture him here in the place that had been all hers, but the garden was very much a retreat and she didn't want memories of him there too. Still, she thought a little more rationally as her logical side stepped up a gear, she could hardly have sprung across the room and hauled him back in the house, could she? And he'd be gone soon, or she could be called out to a case.

As though by command, the telephone began to ring shrilly. After hastily drying her soapy hands, Essie walked across to the small shelf under the window and picked up the receiver.

'Essie?' It was Peter, and never had she been so pleased to hear his voice.

She tried to keep the elation out of hers—Peter would think she had flipped her lid otherwise, she thought wryly—as she said, 'Hi, Peter. Problems?' She was aware of Xavier stepping back inside the house as she spoke; he must have been standing just outside the cottage in the mellow dusky air.

'I'm sorry to call you, Essie—' Peter always started off like that but he didn't mean it. In Peter's book, she and Jamie were lucky to be working for such a reasonable employer and should be prepared to jump at any time, not that Essie minded that '—but Brigadier

Kealey's been on. He's got a lame heifer he'd like someone to look at tonight.'

'All right, I'll go straight up.' The brigadier had a smallholding with just a couple of cows and goats and hens, and his two fine thorough-bred stallions that were his pride and joy. Essie said a quick prayer of gratefulness that it wasn't one of the horses that was ill; they were beautiful animals but highly strung and in-clined to bad temper, and she was very wary of the pair of them.

'Good girl. Call me if you need to.'

Essie could hear the wail of one of Peter's children in the background and Carol's voice calling something, and now she said, her voice wry, 'It sounds as if you've got enough on your plate at home, Peter. I'll see you in the morning.'

She put down the telephone and Xavier's eyes were waiting for her. 'A call out,' he stated flatly.

'I'm afraid so.' Essie was already walking towards the stairs. 'I'll just go get some shoes and a jumper and then I'll have to make tracks. Are you going to be around tomorrow—for that talk?' she added carefully.

'No, I'm not,' he said shortly, the thought of the important meeting he had postponed today when the urge to see her had become overwhelming at the forefront of his mind.

'Oh.' She paused at the bottom of the stairs, looking across at him uncertainly. 'Then perhaps I could ring you tomorrow evening?' she said politely, barely disguising her relief.

She couldn't wait to get rid of him. He felt a surprising and red-hot rage flood him but in the next instant, by a super-human effort, he forced it down and made himself speak normally. 'Possibly.' His voice was clipped. 'You have my number?'

'Yes. Peter gave it to me.'

Essie saw the dark eyebrows rise in enquiry and she added quickly, 'I was going to ring you about the offer—your offer.' She suddenly felt very awkward without really knowing why, and it made her say, as she remembered she was, in essence, the hostess, 'Look, the coffee's ready; there's no reason why you can't have one before you go. Just shut the door after you.'

He nodded slowly. 'A coffee would be most welcome.'

They were back to rigid formality, Essie told herself silently as she ran quickly up the narrow stairs to her bedroom. And why on earth had she suggested he remain in the house after she had gone? Not that she was worried about him poking and prying, or anything like that—that just wasn't Xavier's style. He was too straight and honourable for such behaviour.

Honourable? She caught at the word, pausing for a second as she slipped her canvas shoes on. What was she thinking? she asked herself sharply. She didn't have a clue about what sort of man Xavier was, not really. He could be the most unprincipled man in the world, for all she knew, she warned herself vehemently. She certainly didn't need to start giving him any bouquets, for goodness' sake; no doubt he had more than enough willing females offering him their garlands every day of the week.

He was seated in one of her easy chairs when she hurried down the stairs, a steaming cup of coffee on the floor beside him, and her heart gave a little kick at the sight of him before she took herself in hand, saying coolly, 'Like I said, shut the door after you when you go. It's on the latch.'

'No problem.' He had risen at her approach and now Essie stood rooted in the middle of the room, wondering how best to finish the evening. She was quite unaware of her screaming body language but Xavier read the signs only too well, although his voice betrayed nothing but polite neutrality when he added, 'Goodbye, Essie. I'm sure we'll speak again soon.'

'Yes—yes…right.' Oh, for goodness' sake, don't stutter and stammer, girl, she told herself irritably as she still continued to stand there looking at him. She had expected to have to repel a hug or a kiss—something—and he had completely taken her aback. 'I'll go, then.'

Xavier nodded, the silver-blue eyes as cool as a winter sky, but he didn't speak again. After another moment of awkward silence—at least, on Essie's part—she inclined her head abruptly and walked out of the front door, after picking up her veterinary bag and car keys.

She drove on automatic to the brigadier's house, ten miles away, her mind dissecting every word and gesture she and Xavier had shared until her head was buzzing, and she was heartily glad when the smallholding came into view and she was forced to put her brain into work mode.

At eighteen months old, the heifer was a pretty animal, dark roan in colour and with big liquid eyes that explained the brigadier's name for her—Velvet—but the injury to her foot that was causing her to be lame, with pus seeping onto the straw of her enclosure, had made her nervous.

By the time the heifer had jerked Essie twice against the side of the stable, Essie felt bruised all over, but the worst came when—once the hoof had been scraped and cleaned and made good—Velvet took it into her head to shift position suddenly, her good back hoof grinding down on Essie's left foot. Although Essie had changed her canvas shoes for wellington boots before entering the smallholding, there was little protection from what felt like a ten-ton weight. When she emerged from the stable into the shadowed moonlight she was limping badly.

She left the brigadier billing and cooing over the heifer—the man had a deep affection for all his animals and even his hens died of old age—and hobbled over to the car, reflecting as she did so that she was glad the main thrust of the work at the surgery was with small domestic pets, rather than big beasts like the one she had just dealt with.

Once clear of the smallholding, Essie stopped the car in a pull-in in the quiet country road she was following and inspected the damage to her foot, before surreptitiously easing down her cotton trousers and looking at her leg. Her left side was already a mass of bruises, she reflected soberly, and all her toes were skinned on her left foot and bleeding badly.

'Oh, well, such is life,' she told herself philosophically, before pulling up her trousers over her bruised leg and hip and trying to get her shoe on, which proved more difficult. Her foot was swelling rapidly and was already all the colours of the rainbow.

She sat for some minutes in the quiet of the dark night, the car windows down and the scented summer air stroking over her face. There was the odd cackle and twitter from the huge trees bordering the road which housed an army of birds but, apart from that, the night was quiet and peaceful and Essie drank in the tranquillity in great gulps. But, try as she might, she just couldn't feel that way herself and it annoyed her.

It was him, Xavier Grey, she told herself crossly as she started the car again some five minutes later. Since she had first set eyes on that man nothing had been the same. She sighed confusedly, her mind worrying at the tall, dark spectre that was for ever with her these days.

She hadn't meant to see him again—she hadn't *dreamt* she'd see him again—after that disastrous and acrimonious parting at the hotel on the night of Christine's wedding, but somehow he seemed to have weaved his way into her life and she still wasn't wholly sure how it had happened.

And she didn't want to fancy him. The thought caused her injured foot to jerk on the clutch pedal and she winced as she brought the car to a halt again, only some few hundred yards from where she had been parked before. But she *did* fancy him. She groaned slightly and leant over the steering wheel. She fancied him more than any other man she had ever seen or met, and, worse, much worse, she had even found herself liking him once or twice, before she had brought her mind under control.

Liking him? The words mocked her—they were far too tame to describe the complex emotions tied up with Xavier Grey. Oh, she didn't know *how* she felt, she told herself crossly, and she hated it. She wished he had never looked at her that first time in the church, she wished she'd never responded in the way she had, she wished— She wished a lot of things, and all of them were too darn late.

And now he was seriously considering buying the practice from Peter and suggesting he used the flat as a bolt-hole for when he was in England, and that she and Jamie and possibly a manager run the veterinary surgery beneath, with his blessing. It was…it was absurd, she told herself frantically. Crazy! Mad! It wouldn't work, it *couldn't* work—she would be a nervous wreck within weeks.

She started the engine yet again, her eyes cloudy and miserable. Damn Xavier Grey…

By the time she reached the lane that led to the house, she was stiffening up badly, and Essie's only thought was relaxing in another nice hot bath, so the shock was all the greater when she approached her small pull-in and saw the Mercedes still very firmly in residence.

He was still here? Essie glanced at her watch and saw that two hours had elapsed since her departure. What on earth was he playing at?

She limped towards the house, feeling as though she had been trampled by a herd of bovines rather than just one sweet-faced heifer, and she was just a few feet from the front door when it opened to reveal Xavier in the aperture.

'You're still here.' She didn't wait to reach the cottage to accuse him. 'It's gone midnight.'

'You're limping.' He totally ignored her angry voice. 'What's the matter?'

'Xavier.' She glared at him as she reached the house, hobbling past him when he stood aside for her to enter. 'Why are you still here?' she ground out tightly. 'You said you were going to go.'

'I didn't, actually.' He shut the door and followed her into the sitting room where she had flopped down onto the sofa. 'My going was all your idea.'

Essie surveyed him angrily with simmering blue eyes but Xavier seemed quite oblivious to her rage. 'Why didn't you go?' she asked through gritted teeth.

'Let's see.' He gave her a twist of a smile but there was no answering mellowing on the furious female face looking back at him. 'I could say I fell asleep after the coffee; it's wonderfully relaxing here, without any noise or TV to disturb the peacefulness.'

'*Did* you fall asleep?'

'No.' He eyed her unrepentantly. 'I wanted to stay, that's all. We haven't had our little talk, if you remember, and I think such matters are best dealt with face to face, not over the phone, where lines might get crossed.'

Crossed lines were the least of her troubles.

Essie stared at him and the rugged, dark face stared back at her. She had to apply some tact here—she wouldn't allow herself to term it as cunning—and appeal to his macho gallantry, Essie thought feverishly. She didn't know what Xavier had in mind, but ten to one it wasn't a talk!

'Look, I've had an exhausting evening,' Essie said slowly, and the weariness wasn't all feigned—her left side was hurting like mad and her foot felt twice its size. 'I've been kicked and trampled and I would rather like a soak in a hot bath and then my bed. Could we postpone this?'

'I thought you looked all done in.' Xavier was suddenly solicitous but the brief moment of triumph Essie felt was vanquished when he continued, 'Let's have a look at that foot.' He indicated the red puffy mound spilling over the top of her canvas slip-on.

'No. I can manage perfectly, really.'

Her squeak of protest was ignored as, to Essie's horror, he knelt down in front of her, easing the shoe off her swollen foot with incredible tenderness for such a big man, and then sat back on his heels as he held the discoloured flesh in his hands.

'This is bad.' He cast startled eyes at her and her stomach did a peculiar somersault at the genuine concern in his voice. 'How far does this go up?' He indicated the bruising disappearing into her cotton trousers as he rolled up the material to just below her knee. 'Essie, you're black and blue.'

'It's nothing.' She tried to remove her foot from his grasp but he wouldn't let her and she didn't feel up to a tug of war. 'It's all part of the job.'

'Damn ridiculous job for a woman, if you ask me.' And then, before she could fire back the retort that had sprung to her lips, he said tersely, 'I know, I know; you didn't ask me and I'm every name under the sun. How bad do you feel?'

She actually felt pretty lousy—stiff as a board and the pain was becoming excruciating—but she wasn't about to tell Xavier that. She knew from experience that once she had soaked her bruised and battered flesh in a long hot bath, rubbed on some of the special embrocation which smelt to high heaven and which she kept for just such purposes, and took a couple of strong painkillers, she'd start to feel better.

'I'm all right.'

His narrowed gaze told her exactly what he thought of the lie even before he said, 'Right, I'll run you a bath and then come down and help you up the stairs.'

'You won't, you know.' Essie was beginning to feel horribly trapped and it wasn't a good feeling. 'I can manage perfectly well—good gracious, I have things like this happen all the time and I cope just fine,' she said firmly.

The firmness was like water off a duck's back. 'Here, rest your leg on here.' He moved her around so she was half lying on the sofa, despite her resistance, and had disappeared up the stairs before she could do anything about it.

This was absolutely ridiculous. Essie stared across the sitting room before struggling to her feet as she heard the sound of running water overhead. She didn't *want* him in her bathroom. She didn't want him in her house! Or her life, if it came to that.

The dart of conscience that challenged the validity of the last words made her even more determined to take control again.

He had stayed behind to seduce her, she thought tightly, purposely working up the anger as she limped carefully towards the stairs. She might not go in for the sophisticated games a good few of his women indulged in, but even she knew when she was being hunted! And this was what it boiled down to, at heart. He had stalked her, pursued and hounded her, even when he knew she didn't want anything to do with him.

'What the hell do you think you're doing?' As Essie reached the bottom of the stairs he was there before her, like a great dark avenging angel. Or devil, more like, she amended silently.

'What does it look like?' She glared up at him, but even her anger couldn't disguise the bleached look to her skin induced by the pain.

'It looks like you're being stubborn and stupid,' he shot back grimly. 'It's not a sign of weakness to admit you've taken a hammering tonight, Essie.'

'I know that.' How dared he stand there in the middle of her stairs and tell her what she could and couldn't do? 'But I look after myself three hundred and sixty-five days of the year; what makes tonight any different?' she muttered militantly.

'The fact that I'm here.' His glare matched hers. 'Now, move out of the way.'

As she stood back for him to step into the sitting room, he bent down and swept her up into his arms, ignoring her heated protests as he carried her—with some difficulty, due to the narrow confines of the stairs—to the landing, where he set her down gently.

'I'll check the bath.' He made the minute bathroom in one stride and she stared after him helplessly, feeling utterly out of her depth. Shouldn't he be shooting off round the world securing billion-dollar deals, or whatever else it was that multimillionaires did? she asked herself sourly. She didn't want him here and she didn't need him, either; she was independent—she'd been forced to be that way and now she liked it. *She did.*

With furious determination she ignored the trickles of warmth that were sending little sparks of well-being all over her body, due to his concern, and hobbled over to the bathroom door. 'You can go now.' She peered in at him and felt her stomach constrict as he straightened from the scented bubbly water and turned to face her. 'I'm—'

'Perfectly all right,' he interrupted crisply. 'Yes, you've said.'

'Then why won't you *listen*?'

'Is *that* all right?' He reached out and whisked down her cotton trousers as he spoke, revealing the livid bruising on her left leg in glorious Technicolor. 'And I dare say your hip and side are hurting, too,' he challenged angrily.

'How dare you?' She had never been so surprised and affronted in her life as she faced him with her trousers about her ankles. 'How *dare* you?'

'I dare do much worse than that, believe me,' he ground back irritably, clearly at the end of his tether. 'Now go and get changed for your bath and let's cut the bull, unless you want me to undress you, that is.'

She opened her mouth to argue some more but something in the glittering eyes stopped her. He was quite capable of forcibly undressing her; she could read it in his eyes. 'I hate you.' It was weak, but she had never felt so out of her depth in her life.

'So what's new?'

'No gentleman would have done that,' she mumbled as she bent and pulled up her trousers, her cheeks scarlet.

'And I've never pretended to be one,' he countered evenly. 'Now get in the bedroom and strip off. I'll wait downstairs until you're done. Have you got something for the bruising?'

She nodded sulkily. 'I've still got half a bottle of stuff left over from the last time something like this happened,' she said tightly.

'Then bring it down with you and I'll rub it on,' he said perfectly seriously.

She glanced at him then, edging back towards the bedroom. Over her dead body! He really thought she would lie back and allow him to work the embrocation all over her foot and leg and thigh? It was such a dangerous line of thought that she felt herself going hot.

'And Essie?'

His voice caught her as she made to shut her bedroom door and she paused, peering at him through the crack. 'What?'

'You've got the most beautiful legs I've ever seen,' he said softly, his words starting a fresh riot in her stomach as she continued to stare at him for some seconds more before shutting the door with a definite bang.

CHAPTER SIX

IT WAS a full thirty minutes before Essie gingerly picked her way downstairs again, every bone in her body aching like mad and her left leg and foot feeling as though they were on fire. But it would pass—she knew that. If Xavier would just go, she could take the painkillers and go to bed, she told herself firmly.

'What's that smell?' Xavier wrinkled his nose as she reached the bottom of the stairs, and Essie tried to ignore what the sight of him did to her. He had rolled up his sleeves and undone another couple of buttons of his shirt as he'd stretched out on the sofa and, for some reason, his easy air of relaxed comfort was achingly poignant.

'Embrocation,' she said shortly.

'It smells like the stuff we season wood with, back home.'

'Does it?' She wasn't at all interested in cosy lumberjack reminiscences and her tone stated this quite distinctly. 'Look, Xavier—'

'Come and sit down and I'll make you a hot drink,' he said blandly, as though it were the most normal thing in the world for him to be sitting in her tiny sitting room at one o'clock in the morning.

Essie surveyed him with narrowed blue eyes and tugged the belt of her long thick towelling robe more tightly round her waist. She had dug out her winter pyjamas—bought in the midst of the renovations, when the cottage had been icy-cold—in spite of the muggy June night, feeling her spider-web-thin summer nighties made her a sight too vulnerable with Xavier around; but even with them and her robe she somehow felt too exposed for comfort. 'I really only want to go to bed,' she said firmly.

Tell me about it. Xavier quietened his voice, his tone very gentle as he said, 'I'm due in London first thing for a meeting and then the next two weeks' schedule is punishing. We need to talk now, Essie. I've decided to go ahead with the offer to Peter.'

Just like that. Not that he didn't have the right to do exactly what he wanted with his own money, Essie told herself quickly, but this meant... What did it mean, exactly?

And as though he could read her mind—which Essie wasn't at all sure was too far from the truth—Xavier continued, 'You're obviously wondering how this affects you.'

'Yes, I am,' she said shortly.

'I'll make some coffee.' He waved in invitation towards the sofa—*her* sofa, Essie thought belligerently—as he rose and, simply because there was nothing else she could do, Essie limped across the room and sat down.

'Have you taken anything for the pain?'

She shook her head in answer to his cool, steady voice. 'There are some pills in the top corner cupboard above the kettle,' she said reluctantly. 'I'll have two of them, please.'

There was a long silence while Xavier made the coffee and prepared the tray. It worked on Essie's overwrought nerves like the rasp of fingernails on a blackboard, so it was almost a relief when he came and sat down in the chair opposite her. She didn't want this talk—no, she did want it, she corrected herself confusedly, but not now, not like this.

She looked warily at him and, to her annoyance, he appeared totally at ease, one leg casually crossed over his knee and his torso leaning lazily back in the chair. He also looked broodingly tough and fascinatingly sexy, she thought as her heart thudded and then began to pound away like a sledgehammer. There was an aura of leashed sensuality about him, a disturbingly male warmth that suggested that, once he dropped the cloak of cool remoteness that seemed to sit on the powerful shoulders like an invisible force, it would reveal pure dynamite.

Essie forced her mind back to the matter in hand, taking a deep hidden breath before she managed to say, 'I don't understand why you would want to buy the practice, Xavier. Surely there must be other properties nearer to your place of business that are more suitable?' There, that was the right note to hit, she thought with some satisfaction—cool, controlled and very matter-of-fact.

He shrugged slowly. 'It depends on your definition of suitable,' he drawled quietly. 'Due to certain business developments in the last few years, I find I am spending more and more time in England, and that is likely to increase, not decrease. However, I have my home in Canada with Candy, and even when she gets married I would be loath to move elsewhere.

'I've spent a fortune on hotels in the last few years and I hate hotel living at the best of times, added to which an apartment in the city does not appeal. Put it down to the wide open spaces in Canada, but I find cities claustrophobic.'

Essie nodded. She could well understand that—she felt exactly the same herself.

'Peter's property is a beautiful old house and the location is perfect for my needs,' Xavier continued, looking at her lazily with hooded eyes which revealed absolutely nothing. 'The flat conversion is both sensitive and spacious, and as I shall be using the place only when I'm in England any property I might buy or rent would be vacant for half the year, with all the attendant problems regarding security. With the surgery operating downstairs during the day and the small flat over the garages already available for a live-in veterinary—and you and Jamie would need someone else, to replace Peter—that problem is negated.'

Essie stared at him as her mind raced. She'd forgotten about the two-roomed flat—which was virtually a bedsit—above the double garage at the back of the house. Peter had lived there while the house was being converted, before Carol had joined him, but once their home was ready the two rooms above the garage had been used for storage and all but forgotten. But now it seemed Xavier planned to resurrect the tiny home.

She drew in air between her teeth, bending down for her coffee mug and taking a long gulp at the hot, fragrant liquid as she searched her mind frantically for good reasons why his proposal was flawed. There weren't any. At least, not on his side. On *her* side... Oh, what was she going to say? What was she going to *do*?

'And this way you get to keep your job and your home.'

The words, spoken as they were in a very soft Canadian drawl, nevertheless had the effect of a dousing of cold water on Essie. Her head jerked upright, her mouth falling open in a little gape before she shut it with a snap.

'You're not doing this for me, I hope,' she bit back sharply, her eyes hostile. It was as she'd thought all along: he was trying to blackmail her into sleeping with him. It was as plain as the nose on his face, she thought furiously. And for a minute there she'd almost believed...

'Would that be such a terrible thing?' Xavier asked dispassionately, his eyes watching her very closely in spite of his apparent detachment. 'Is it really so unthinkable that you and Jamie should benefit from my finding the perfect property for my needs?'

Put like that, it wasn't, of course—but he hadn't mentioned Jamie a moment or two ago.

'And the veterinary side of things is a very lucrative business.' Xavier smiled, but she didn't trust his smile any more than she trusted him. 'And I'm a businessman first and foremost.'

She wasn't sure what he was first and foremost, but this whole proposal was distinctly suspicious. Essie was struggling with the mounting effects of an exhausting day, an even more exhausting evening—and she didn't necessarily put the incident with the heifer at the head of that, either—and the weakening sleepiness the strong painkillers were inducing, but she didn't dare relax for a second.

'You'd have to get someone in to do the office work, with Carol going,' she said tightly, 'and that's a huge task.'

'It's not so big.' His smile this time was merely a twitch and his voice was soothing—patronisingly so, Essie thought viciously.

'There are a hundred and one panics every day—'

'Essie, you've done nothing at all but tell me how capable and proficient and independent you are, since the day we met,' Xavier interrupted briskly. 'Prove it.'

She loathed this man. Essie looked down at the mug clasped in her hands as she searched for fresh ammunition, fighting the heaviness that was aiming to close her eyelids. And when she next raised her head he had moved closer, his mouth just inches from hers. She gazed at him, mesmerised, and then his big frame was next to her on the sofa and his mouth was touching her drooping eyelids in gentle, delicate kisses that caused her head to fall back languorously against the cushions.

'So fierce, so brave...' The light stroking became sweeter as his lips moved to hers, and when her mouth opened beneath the warm, knowing assault he plunged swiftly into the newly won territory, causing Essie to begin to tremble at the heady rush of sensation his lovemaking had induced.

Somehow she found her hands had lifted to his shoulders as he half knelt over her, intent on the gentle eroticism his mouth and hands were accomplishing, and she shivered at the feel of his hard bunched muscles beneath the thin material of his shirt.

He tasted wonderful. The thought was there, but it was only one of myriad swirling feelings and perceptions that deepened into a tingling whole. And he felt wonderful, too. He was locked onto her now, breath for breath, and his thighs were alien and powerful against the softness of her body. He moved, pressing her further into the cushions of the sofa—and suddenly the pain from her injured side was there, causing her to wince against his lips.

'Hell, I'm sorry.'

She was instantly free and she felt horribly bereft as she opened dazed eyes to see him kneeling over her again, his eyes rueful. 'You're sore all over and ready to drop,' he said softly. 'You're right. We'll talk some more another time.'

No, no, she wasn't that sore. For an awful moment Essie thought she had blurted the words out loud, but when his face didn't change she knew she had been spared that final humiliation.

It took another few moments for her to pull herself together, but by the time Xavier had straightened and stood up she had mastery over the feverish desire to beg him to start making love to her again. Which would have been crazy, utterly hare-brained, she told herself grimly. Physical attraction was one thing, love was another, and to Essie sexual fulfilment had to go hand in hand with the last commodity. Xavier wasn't in love with her and she wasn't in love with him, and that was the bottom line.

The next morning Essie was feeling even more stiff and bone-tired after a restless night filled with pain and strange nightmarish dreams the pills had conjured up, but unutterably glad she had nothing more to reproach herself for as far as Xavier was concerned than allowing him to kiss her.

The man didn't know the first thing about emotional commitment, she told herself firmly as she lowered her aching body into a hot, steaming bath first thing. And she didn't want any sort of obligation or tie to a man—that was the last thing on earth she wanted! Of course it was.

Colin Fulton had been a nice normal human being until he had married her mother, and then all hell had been let loose as the devil beneath the façade of angel had been revealed. And her mother had been trapped—or had thought she was trapped, anyway—and so the cycle of physical violence and beatings and mental cruelty had begun.

And Andrew. He had sworn love and devotion and a number of other things whilst sleeping with anyone who would give him bed room. And she hadn't known. Essie's teeth gritted together as an echo of the shame and self-abasement she had felt all those years ago made her shut her eyes tightly before opening them wide.

Of course Xavier wasn't Colin or Andrew, she knew that, and he had been quite open about his track record with the opposite sex without glossing over the facts. But just at the moment she wasn't sure if that made her feel better or worse. Which was all the more confusing. And she didn't want to feel confused. She didn't want to feel bewildered and on edge and always at sixes and sevens, either, all of which she'd been feeling constantly since the first time she had set eyes on him.

She soaked her sore, tense muscles for ten minutes in the therapeutic warmth of the water, and when she climbed gingerly out of the bath she found she felt heaps better, although her left side—from hip to foot—bore all the colours of the spectrum.

Xavier *had* been very concerned about her last night. As Essie pulled on a pair of comfortably loose-fitting trousers and a short-sleeved top, the thought came from nowhere and caused her to pause, the kingfisher-blue crêpe top half over her head. *None of that!* She jerked the top right down and stared at her face in the long rectangle of mirror she had fixed to the bedroom wall.

She knew the ulterior motive behind the kindness—she wasn't stupid or that naive, she told the anxious-faced reflection in the mirror. All his revelations about his childhood and Candy and the rest didn't alter the fact that he was a wolf in—what? Sheep's clothing? No, a wolf in wolf's clothing would be more apt where Xavier was concerned, Essie admitted soberly. He didn't disguise what he was and he wasn't ashamed of it either.

Still, he was gone now—at least for a couple of weeks. The thought should have brought relief and satisfaction at the very least, but instead the vague feeling of depression she had woken up with deepened. It was the pills. Essie nodded to herself before squeezing her flat open-toed sandal over her swollen foot and doing up the buckle on the last hole. It was definitely the pills. She hated taking painkillers and rarely did—all those chemicals and goodness knew what *had* to have an adverse effect—but they'd been necessary last night.

She left the cottage half an hour before her usual time so she could take a nice leisurely drive over the short distance to the surgery, and then get herself installed without any rush or fuss. She couldn't hurry this morning, not with every nerve twanging.

It was a beautiful morning and the scent of roses and pinks and catmint was heavy in the air as she stepped out of the front door into the small front garden, the hum of bees indicating there were others who had risen before her.

Essie stood for a moment, her eyes lifting to the bright blue arch of the sky and the perfume of summer filling her nostrils as she thought, Where is he, I wonder? Right now?

This time the alarm bell rang loudly enough to wake the dead. She shouldn't be giving any thoughts of Xavier Grey house room, she told herself vehemently—not those sorts of thoughts, anyway! She had only known him a short time and he had turned her world upside down and forced himself into her life with all the delicacy of a bulldozer—despite the veneer of smooth constraint that covered all his actions.

He was dangerous. He was so, so dangerous, and never had she seen so clearly that, compared to Xavier, Colin and Andrew were purring pussycats. Because there was something about Xavier—some deep attraction, an almost hypnotising magnetism—that could seep into a woman's blood like an addictive drug until her mind couldn't think of anything else and her body was craving his touch. But not *this* woman.

Up till now, he had had things all his own way. Essie breathed in the clean, light-washed air as her brain raced on. She knew nothing about him except what he had chosen to tell her—she didn't even know where his business in England was located—and perhaps it was time to make some enquiries of her own. She nodded at the thought.

She'd be discreet, of course, but Christine and Charlie were just back from honeymoon now and if she could get her friend to pump her new husband on all he knew... Yes, that was the way to go. Somehow this whole thing had got utterly out of hand and she needed to feel in control of her destiny again.

She straightened her shoulders, the frown lifting from her face. Operation Xavier Grey was about to commence.

CHAPTER SEVEN

IT WAS later that afternoon when the fragrant bouquet of roses and freesias was delivered to the practice, along with a small card which read, 'The beast in question couldn't express its regret at its churlishness so I've taken the liberty.' It was simply signed 'X'.

Essie stared at the flowers for some thirty seconds when Carol placed them in her hands, gushing loudly, and the tumultuous emotions that washed over her strengthened—rather than weakened—her resolve to do some homework on Xavier.

Six days later, it was an exquisitely worked small porcelain figure of a tiny milkmaid milking a cow—which must have cost a small fortune—and this time he'd written, 'As the saying goes, I saw this and thought of you. X.' The package had been sent from Germany—where she assumed he must be—but any warm feelings Essie might have felt were kept rigidly under control. Her enquiries had had results and she was flaming mad.

A full two weeks after she had last seen Xavier—and the day after she had thrown out the last of the wilting roses and freesias—an enchanting basket of delicately perfumed orchids made their appearance. This time the card made her sit down very suddenly. 'See you soon, X.'

See you soon. But after what she had found out about Xavier Grey he wasn't going to get quite the reception he had been angling for, Essie told herself grimly, refusing to acknowledge the way her heart had leapt at the sight of the strong, black and very male scrawl.

But she wasn't thinking of Xavier at four o'clock that afternoon when she drove into the practice's drive. She was still wrapped in the warm afterglow of the successful home visit she had just paid in answer to a desperate phone call three hours earlier.

Mrs Bloomsbury—a little old lady who lived in a neat, picturesque thatched cottage a few miles away, and whose life revolved around her small Jack Russell, Ginny—had called to say that Ginny's confinement wasn't going to plan and she was worried she couldn't have the puppies naturally.

As soon as Essie had seen the little creature panting miserably in her basket she had known Mrs Bloomsbury was right—there was a problem—and her careful examination had shown there was what felt like an enormous pup wedged firmly inside the birth canal.

However, some delicate assistance with the help of forceps and an injection of pituitrin had seen the big puppy delivered safe and well, with another hefty bruiser following twenty minutes later, and a smaller pup fifteen minutes after that.

By the time Essie had left the now beaming Mrs Bloomsbury, Ginny's new family were feeding well and the little dog was looking extremely proud of herself, as well she might. The two male puppies were enormous for such a small dog.

Essie's last sight of the small brood had been a happy one—Ginny was obviously going to be a devoted mother and the smaller female puppy was determined not to be outdone by her burly brothers in the food stakes. All in all a great afternoon, Essie reflected contentedly.

The Mercedes was sitting much as it had done that first time some weeks before, its gleaming exterior and regal lines proclaiming its separation from the common herd, and the sight of it swept away Essie's elation as though it had never been.

Xavier. She gripped the steering wheel so hard, the white of her knuckles showed.

Well, she knew it had had to come and perhaps it was better to get the confrontation over with as quickly as she could. But this was going to upset everyone in some way or another, although at least Jamie's job was relatively secure now.

Peter had mentioned that he had accepted Xavier's offer for the business and the house the day she had received the first bouquet, and she understood the deal was progressing smoothly.

Essie entered the house quietly, making her way through to the kitchen past the reception area and the two consulting rooms after saying hello to Marion, the middle-aged woman who was in charge of Reception from half-past eight to six every day. Once in the kitchen she was relieved to find it empty—Jamie had been called out after they had finished morning surgery and had left before she'd gone to Mrs Bloomsbury's and she was glad he wasn't back yet. She didn't want to have to talk to anyone.

She switched on the kettle and made herself a strong black instant coffee, drinking it straight down, scalding hot, as she took stock of how to proceed.

And then she whirled round as though she had been shot as a cool, laconic voice behind her said, 'Hi there.'

'Hello.' Two bright spots of colour burned on her cheekbones as Essie forced herself to meet Xavier's silver-blue gaze. She saw that, although he was smiling, the narrowed eyes were unreadable. 'I saw the car,' she said stiffly, making herself speak more to prove to Xavier that she wasn't tongue-tied by his presence than anything else.

He nodded slowly without taking his eyes off her. 'I was with Peter,' he said shortly. And then, as they continued to look at each other, he asked, 'How are you feeling? The bruising settled down?'

'I'm fine, thank you.' She ought to thank him for the flowers and the figurine, she told herself desperately, but in view of what she had to say it just didn't seem appropriate. Nevertheless, she took a deep breath and said, her voice tense, 'The flowers and the little milkmaid were very kind of you, but you shouldn't have; I didn't expect anything like that.'

'I know you didn't.' She was as tight as a coiled spring and instinct told him it was something more than the usual wariness she displayed around him. Xavier took a deep breath of his own and took the bull by the horns. 'What's the matter?' he asked evenly.

'Why did you lie to me?' The words came out flat and bald but he didn't react by so much as the flicker of an eyelash, she noticed with burning resentment. 'You already have a penthouse in London, don't you?' she accused more hotly.

So that was it. He should have known she'd find out—in fact he *had* known, he acknowledged silently. He'd just hoped it wouldn't be too soon. But he should have expected it. Essie was Essie. 'I didn't lie to you,' he said coolly.

'Yes, you did. Charlie's mother knows you have an apartment—'

'I'm not denying I have a place elsewhere,' he interrupted tersely, 'but I didn't lie to you. I *have* spent a fortune on hotels in my time, which is why I got the apartment, and it is useful in its own way. However, I don't like city life—as I told you before—and so somewhere like this is very pleasant as a bolt-hole when needed.'

A bolt-hole when needed? Essie couldn't remember when she'd last felt so mad. She'd been called a lot of things in her time, but a bolt-hole was a first. 'Are you selling the penthouse?' she asked tightly.

'No, I am not,' he answered just as tightly, his tone indicating it was nothing to do with her one way or the other. 'It is extremely useful for entertaining business colleagues and is an excellent base for my purposes when I am working.'

'Then why have you bought this place?' Essie retorted. As if she didn't know. A mistress in a bolt-hole. It sounded like something out of a bad novel, she thought a trifle hysterically.

'For relaxing.' He was trying hard to keep his temper. 'Everyone needs to relax sometimes, Essie, or didn't you know?'

'Relaxing!' It was scathing. 'You must think I was born yesterday.'

For a moment, one of the cutting and cruel remarks he was so good at was there in his mind, but then he looked into her face—really looked into it—and he saw the fear and defiance she was trying to hide. And it did something to him. Something he didn't want to examine and had certainly not bargained for. But it also told him if he didn't go with the flow now he had no hope of any sort of relationship with this woman in the future.

And he wanted her. Even now, in the midst of all this, just looking at her made his blood run like hot mulled wine.

'You're asking me why I bought Peter's home and business,' Xavier said very slowly, 'and I've told you one of the reasons—although I admit it is not the main one.'

He paused, aware she was watching him in the same way an injured animal caught in a trap watched someone approach them—not at all sure of their motives but ready to bite and scratch and fight to the death, if need be.

'I bought this place mainly because of you.' He held up his hand as she went to speak, her eyes fiery. 'No, give me a chance to finish, Essie,' he said sharply.

He saw her chin jerk upwards and her mouth clench but at least she kept quiet.

'You think I want you and you are dead right; I do. I've wanted you from the first second I laid eyes on you, before I knew who you were or what you were like; but since I've got to know you I want you more and more.' He was watching the impact of his words register in the beautiful violet eyes. 'I followed you down here because I couldn't get you out of my mind and I wanted to find out what made you tick,' he continued swiftly. 'And then I discovered that in all probability you are about to lose your job and maybe, as a consequence of that, your home.'

'And of course there was poor Jamie, too,' Essie said derisively, forcing the sarcasm out of the whirling confusion she was feeling.

He called on his considerable will-power and made himself smile slowly. 'I don't want to sleep with Jamie, Essie,' he said with a dry mockery directed at himself.

He saw her eyes widen with surprise as she recognised the self-disparagement but then, in the next instant, the wariness took over, stronger than before. She was so full of distrust, it was like solid armour.

'So you are buying the practice and the business and everything so you can sleep with me?' It was what she had suspected all along but she still found it astounding.

'That would be the icing on the cake, but if it doesn't happen it doesn't happen,' Xavier said with an ease that belied the endless cold showers of the last weeks. 'I don't expect you to drop your principles along with a certain item of your underwear, if that's what you're asking. I'm attracted to you, I'd like to get to know you more and then—if things work out, of course—I'd like us to become more than just friends; but that would depend purely on you. I've never yet forced a woman to sleep with me and I don't intend to start with you.'

She stared at him, absolutely at a loss as to what to say next. This was all so incredible, so…un-English! She licked her dry lips—conscious of his eyes following the action—and then managed, 'So you're insisting it's not blackmail?'

'Ugly word,' he said grimly.

'It's an ugly deed.'

'Essie, I'm going to tell you something,' Xavier said very softly, but something in his tone made her eyes narrow.

'What?' she asked warily, struggling for calmness.

'It's nothing to do with this situation—not in essence, anyway—but it might explain something of where I'm coming from.' He indicated one of the kitchen stools with a wave of his hand as he leant against the far wall, thrusting his hands deep into the pockets of his trousers as he surveyed her coolly from under half-lowered lids.

The entirely natural pose emphasised his dark virility to the point where Essie wanted to leap on him—it quite literally made her knees weak—and, as much to retain her dignity as anything else, she made herself perch on the stool before her legs gave out.

'I've told you about my mother. She left England pregnant by a man who was not her husband—he was her husband's best friend, as it happens, but that's another story—and that guy didn't stay around for long after Natalie was born. Our name became a byword where she lived and when Natalie was raped the cops virtually shut their eyes to it—like mother, like daughter, was the response we got. Natalie was a sweet, gentle kid and she didn't have a grain of my mother's weakness in her, but what the heck? A Grey was a Grey was a Grey, as far as they were concerned.'

Essie stared at him. She didn't want to hear this—she didn't want him to have to tell it—but for his sake, not hers, and that in itself was scary.

'I was working at fifteen and by eighteen I was beginning to make good money—more money than any of the college kids could hope to make when they graduated. I worked twenty-four hours a day when it was necessary, because I was determined to make good; I'd found something I was good at, you know?'

Essie nodded slowly. Yes, she knew. It was exactly how she had felt when she'd realised her passion was veterinary work.

'And I met a girl,' he said flatly. He turned from her at this point, his eyes looking past her to the open window which overlooked Peter's square of back garden which had been made into a car park for the surgery's customers, and so he didn't see her wince.

But Essie felt it. And it horrified her. She didn't care if he had loved someone, she told herself vehemently. It was *nothing* to do with her.

'Well, I guess it's wrong to say I "met" Bobbie,' he continued expressionlessly. 'I'd known her all my life, in a remote way. She was the daughter of the local mayor and she was the same age as me, but hers had been a privileged upbringing. She'd been the Beauty Pageant Queen, the Prom Queen—you name it...' He paused, and Essie found she was hardly breathing.

'We started dating. I was pretty green, in those days, but I knew I wasn't the first guy she'd had. But I didn't care; I was in love and she was my first and it felt great. And then she took me home one day to meet her folks.'

He turned to look at her then, shrugging slightly as he said, 'They were all charm until she said my name and then they went ape. Her brothers took me out onto the front lawn and they beat the hell out of me.'

'But didn't she try to stop them?' Essie whispered softly. 'And what about her parents?'

'Her father was the one directing the punches,' Xavier said with a touch of dark humour. 'It was the typical ''don't darken my door again'' line, and Bobbie went along with them—or, at least, she didn't care enough to try and stop it. I told myself she was just frightened and I tried a hundred times to see her, until she got one of her friends to spell it out. I was born on the wrong side of the tracks and she didn't want to see me again.'

'Oh, Xavier.' She looked at him, the frighteningly sensual good looks and dark, magnetic, powerful appeal so strong it was lethal, and wondered how this Bobbie could have thrown away such a prize.

'And then, in the next few months, two things happened,' he said levelly. 'My mother died and I had the sort of break that comes once in a lifetime and I grabbed it with both hands. Before I knew where I was, I was on my way to making my first million, and in the small town where I'd grown up that was big news. Suddenly I was the guy everyone wanted to know. I'd just moved Candy and me and a live-in housekeeper into a new house when Bobbie and her father turned up one night.'

Xavier shook his head at the memory, standing up straight and rotating his big shoulders before he said, 'It appeared she was pregnant and, according to them, I was the father. Never mind I hadn't laid eyes—or anything else—on her for months.'

'What did you do?' It was a stupid question. Knowing Xavier as she did, she knew exactly what he would have done.

'I told them to get the hell out of my house.' Even now, his voice held some satisfaction at the memory. 'And then Bobbie's father turned nasty. Threatened to mess up my future—he knew a lot of people—if I didn't play ball and take on Bobbie.'

'And?'

'He tried the blackmail for a couple of weeks and then Bobbie came in with the emotional stuff.' His voice held all the warmth of splintered ice. 'When they saw I wasn't going to budge, they did their worse. It got…grubby. I knew the guy Bobbie had been dating. He'd just gone to university and his parents were wealthy—all garden parties and tennis in the afternoons—and it was clear neither he nor his parents had bargained for a young wife hanging round his neck.'

'There was no chance the baby was yours?' She had to ask.

'Not unless you believe in thirteen-month pregnancies.' Xavier's voice was cool and steady.

'Did you do anything?'

'Try to prove my innocence, you mean?' His voice was very dry and caustic. 'Me? Xavier Grey? And who the hell would have believed me against the local mayor's blue-eyed darling? No, I sat it out and, once the baby was born, I insisted on a blood test. That was an experience.' His mouth twisted. 'But it proved Bobbie's child wasn't mine and I made sure the news was broadcast on the front page of the local paper. Who says money doesn't have its advantages?' he said with a bright, shark-like smile.

Yes, she could imagine Xavier would want his pound of flesh, Essie thought with painful insight. She could also see how such an experience would have hardened and further wounded an already badly damaged young man, turning him into the cynical and sardonic man of the present.

'So…' His eyes were tight on her as she sat motionless on the stool. 'Trust me on this, if nothing else, Essie. I wouldn't blackmail you into crossing the road, let alone sleeping with me. When I have you, it will be because you want it every bit as much as I do.'

'When you have me?' It should have been indignant and icy—that was how she wanted her voice to sound—but instead it came out breathless and faint.

'When I have you,' he affirmed gratingly. And then he walked across to her slowly, taking his time, and pulled her off the stool and into his arms.

She was wearing her flat canvas shoes and her head only came to his shoulders, but instead of his height and breadth being threatening—something she had always felt in the past, because Colin had been a big man and had used his male strength to every advantage against the rest of the household—it was exhilarating.

He curved an arm about her slender waist, drawing her closer into him, and the remembered smell of him enfolded her, enticing her heightened senses.

But he didn't kiss her as she was expecting. Instead he looked down at her, his eyes holding hers in a ray of silver light that was impossible to look away from. 'So what about you?' he said softly. 'You know all about me, but what turned you into the woman you are?'

'The woman I am?' Essie suddenly found she didn't like the way things were going and tried to pull away, but her resistance was ignored. 'You don't know anything about me.'

'Ain't that the truth?' he drawled mockingly. 'But what I do know is so paradoxical as to be ridiculous. You are ravishingly beautiful—' she tried to pull away harder but it was like pushing against immovable steel '—and have the sort of figure that could drive a man wild; you're twenty-eight years of age, unattached, and devoted to your career. Now all that would be just fine if there was a man around somewhere, or if there had been a man around in the last little while. But according to Enoch's mother—who had it on good authority from Christine's mother—you haven't dated in years. Why?'

Damn family gossip. Essie knew her cheeks were burning and she tilted her chin as she said, 'That's absolutely nothing to do with you.'

'This guy who hurt you—it was really that bad?' Xavier asked softly, and suddenly all the mockery was gone and his voice resembled thick warm chocolate.

She couldn't do this. She knew he must be able to feel the tension that had snaked through every nerve and sinew, but she couldn't help it; his gentleness was making her want to cry. She stared at him, still wrapped in his arms and so close she could see where his stubble was beginning to grow back after his shave that morning. And his eyelashes, he had incredibly thick, curling eyelashes for a man, she thought helplessly. Oh, dammit. *Dammit.*

'It's not like you think,' she said at last, her voice little more than a whisper.

'You don't know what I think.' You don't know how this thing has haunted me—the images I've had in my mind when I dare to let my mind wander and imagine what that swine might have done to you... A host of questions hovered on his lips but he didn't know if he had the guts to face the possible answers. Him, Xavier Grey, well-known ruthless so-and-so and tough guy, he mocked himself mordantly. But this was different.

Unbidden, a memory came back to him of a slender, sweet-faced girl curled up on her mother's bed where she had been carried by the brute who had forced her. He had found Natalie there when he had come back late one evening from baseball practice. She had been bruised and bleeding and he didn't think the image would ever fade from his mind. His mother had been slumped in an armchair in their grimy living room and she had been blind drunk, the man long since gone.

He had walked the streets for hours with his baseball bat once Natalie was asleep, looking for a man fitting the description his sister had given him, but of course he hadn't found him.

'I don't want to talk about it.' This time Essie's voice was firmer.

'Okay.' It was immediate and he took her by surprise again; she hadn't thought he would acquiesce so easily. Her face must have spoken for her because, in the next moment, he nuzzled the top of her head with his chin as he said huskily, 'I don't know him, but I want to kill him because he's hurt you. I don't know if that will make it easier or harder for you to tell me what went wrong, in the future.'

He raised his head and looked into her eyes again and for several seconds—seconds that stretched and tautened until both of them were scarcely breathing—she held the silver gaze.

The future. He was talking as though *they* had a future, Essie thought as the panic hit, and immediately she lowered her lashes, her voice trembling slightly as she said, 'I...I need to go. There are things I must do.'

'I know just how you feel.'

His lips were warm and firm against hers as he kissed her, and he took his time, leaving her mouth every so often to drop little kisses on her eyelids and her forehead and her cheeks until he felt her begin to relax against him.

Her hair was silky and smelt of apples and her skin was like warm honey, and Xavier found it the most difficult thing in his life so far not to rush her.

But she deserved better than that, he told himself with rigid control. Whatever had happened to her had caused her to retreat into herself, to become self-sufficient, but unhealthily so. Maybe he recognised that in her because there was an element of the same thing in himself? Not on the physical side of things—his was more of a mind independence, a desire to be self-governing and emotionally uncommitted—but women were different. Their mind-set about the act of love was different.

The thought disturbed him and he immediately dismissed it. She knew exactly where he was coming from—he'd made it clear from the beginning he wasn't the marrying kind; but then, neither was she. Her career was the pivot of her life.

'Xavier…' Essie was kissing him back now and the control was harder to keep up.

He explored the pure line of her throat with his lips and she moaned softly. He stroked the soft fullness of her breasts and felt them harden to peaks beneath the thin top she was wearing, and she gasped out loud.

Had that guy been the first? In a strange way, Xavier found himself hoping he hadn't been. He didn't like to think that the only experience she had had of sexual fulfilment had been something that had ended so badly, perhaps even violently. He pushed the thought from him and pulled her harder into him so he could feel the whole length of her body against his frame, hating the fact that—perversely—he didn't like to think of another man touching her, loving her, whether he'd been as gentle as a kitten or not. Crazy and illogical. The razor-sharp brain made the analysis and so dismissed that line of thought as unacceptable.

Their kisses were deeper and hungrier now and, although Xavier was holding her hard against him, Essie was clinging to him every bit as hard.

They both heard the back door that led into the customers' car park bang, followed by

Jamie's unmistakable whistle, but for a moment neither of them reacted. And then Essie pushed him away, her breath coming in frantic gasps, and turned blindly towards the sink unit.

'Coffee.' It was an unsteady, high squeak, and she cleared her throat, saying, just before the door to the kitchen opened, 'I'll make some coffee,' a little more coherently.

She busied herself filling the kettle as Jamie entered, returning his cheerful greeting over her shoulder as she added, 'I'm making some coffee, Jamie. You want one?'

Xavier's deep, controlled voice was exactly the same as usual, Essie noted somewhat resentfully as she fiddled about with mugs and sugar until she felt sufficiently composed to turn and face the room where the two men were now deep in conversation. And he looked the same as usual. There wasn't a thing to suggest that, just a few minutes before, they had been locked in a passionate embrace and he had wanted her. But he had—his body had provided ample proof of that.

The thought turned her cheeks pink again and she was relieved when, the kettle having boiled and the coffees made—and without once having met Xavier's gaze—she was able to make a dignified exit from the room, pleading a couple of urgent things to do before evening surgery.

Once outside in the hall, she scurried along to the safe sanctuary of the downstairs cloakroom, locking the door behind her and then walking over to the washbasin as she stared into the fixed round mirror above it.

Her face was warm and glowing and her eyes were bright, and her lips—Essie shut her eyes tightly. Her lips looked as though they had been well and truly kissed.

She wasn't ready for any of this. Suddenly the elation vanished and she dropped her head against the smooth, cold glass, tears scalding the backs of her eyes. She didn't think she'd ever be ready for it. She wasn't the type of person who could go into an affair with her eyes wide open, knowing it had absolutely no chance of lasting. And this hadn't. Xavier had never pretended any different on that score.

She bit on her lower lip, opening her eyes again and then splashing her face with cold water until her skin was numb. She dried her face slowly, running her fingers through her curls and restoring her hair to something like tidiness. And then she sat for long minutes on the small straight-backed chair the little room boasted, willing herself to think sensibly.

She couldn't handle an affair with Xavier and she would run a mile if he suggested anything more permanent, she admitted honestly—not that he would, of course. And why? Because she was terrified of committing herself to any man ever again. She didn't trust that things wouldn't change or that there wasn't a hidden agenda; that was it, at bottom. Which left her...?

She wrinkled her brow and stood up abruptly, irritated with herself and Xavier and the world in general. In no-man's land, that was where it left her. And things had been so *normal* before she'd met Xavier. She'd worked hard and got what she wanted and the future had looked rosy, and she deserved that—she did!

She sucked in air between her teeth, smoothing down her jeans over her hips with thoughtful hands. This wasn't all her, not really; part of it was Xavier, too. He wasn't the sort of man that you could ever forget on just an everyday level, but to have a love affair with him... He would eat her up and spit her out and not even notice. You didn't get over someone like Xavier; the most you could hope for was to learn to live with the pain when he said goodbye, and she didn't want that. She *wouldn't* have that.

But now he was buying the practice, and things were complicated and messy and muddled. Darn it. She shook her head, her eyes cloudy. But she would have to tell him how she felt. It was the only way.

It was half-past six when Essie finished evening surgery and, as she had expected, Xavier was still around. Jamie had told her Xavier and Peter were finalising the last details on the purchase of the house and business and that Peter already had a provisional date to leave England. It didn't help the panic that kept washing over her at regular intervals.

'Can I give you a lift home?' Xavier popped his head round her consulting-room door two moments after the last patient had gone.

'I've got my own car, thanks. I always bring it if I'm on house-calls, although if it's Jamie's or Peter's turn and I get called out there's always the spare car—Peter's old Mini. I don't really like to drive that, though, and—'

He interrupted her incoherent babbling by the simple expedient of speaking her name, his voice low and deep.

'Don't.' She turned to him then, her face wretched.

'Why?' he asked calmly.

'You really want to know?'

He nodded slowly.

'Okay.' And so she told him exactly how she felt, as she had planned to do earlier, and he listened quietly, his face expressing nothing.

'And that's it?'

She stared at him, uncertain of where he was coming from. 'Xavier, I've just said I don't want to get involved with you,' she said carefully, 'and I shan't change my mind. If you're going to buy this property thinking it will be any different, it won't.'

'Fine.' He regarded her imperturbably, his voice remote. 'No problem. We'll just be friends, then.'

'Friends don't kiss the way you kissed me earlier,' Essie said tightly, summoning all her courage as she did so.

'That's a point.' He smiled at her, his eyes as silver as a shaft of moonlight, and again his magnetism reached out and caused every nerve in her body to tingle. 'No more kisses, then?'

She shook her head, her face resolute.

'Shame.' There was a trickle of something in the husky tones that made her shiver and she hoped he hadn't noticed. 'Real, real shame—but if that's the way you want it...'

'It is.'

'So, friends and working colleagues, then.'

'Working colleagues?' She blinked at him. Why did she always feel she was one step forward and two steps back in any sort of conversation with this man?

'Obviously with Peter going and the appointment of a new veterinary and office clerk, things will change round here,' Xavier said evenly. 'I intend to run this practice as a money-making venture but, as I shan't be around on a day-to-day basis, things need to be set in operation from day one.'

Essie blinked again.

'To that end, I've a proposal to put to you,' Xavier said smoothly, 'over dinner. A friendly dinner. In a restaurant with hundreds of other people present, if it makes you feel better.'

He needn't make her out to be some sort of pathetic nut, Essie thought grimly, forcing herself not to snap as she said, 'You mean to-night?'

'I sure do.'

'All right.' The least she could do was hear what he had to say, after he'd taken her rejection of any intimacy between them so well. 'I'll...I'll meet you later. Where and what time?'

'Friends don't pick other friends up?'

She shook her head, hating his amused smile as he said, 'Half-past eight, the Willow Pond Hotel.'

'I'll be there.' She tried to inject some briskness into her voice.

'Good.' He thought about how she had felt, pressed against him earlier, and his body responded instantly. 'I'll look forward to it,' he said blandly.

'Are Peter and Jamie coming?'

He stared at her, his eyes unblinking and very direct. 'I think you know the answer to that.'

She had known the answer and she wasn't quite sure why she had asked the question in the first place. Perhaps it was because she didn't like his easy acceptance of the new status quo? The thought was shocking but it was also true, and Essie had never been one to duck and dive when faced with the facts.

'But it's a business dinner?' she pressed tenaciously, her stubbornness directed against her own secret longings if he had but known it.

'It is.' And then he stepped forward and kissed her lightly on the mouth, turning away as he said, 'A business dinner between one friend who needs to talk privately to another friend. Okay? And Essie…?'

He had reached the front door and he opened it, turning in the aperture and looking at her where she stood, one hand pressed to her mouth, before he drawled, 'I always kiss my friends goodbye like that—the female ones, anyway. You know us Canadians: friendly bunch.'

'You're the only Canadian I know,' she managed fairly steadily, considering her heart was going haywire.

'Is that so?'

He looked impossibly attractive standing there, Essie thought helplessly. Attractive and hard and so totally sure of himself that it was terrifying. And after all he had been through— the horror of his childhood and the fight to get where he was now—was it any wonder he was so tough? But he could be gentle. Gentle and wonderfully tender. She slammed the door shut on that particular avenue of thought before her traitorous mind got her into trouble, and her voice was deliberately light when she said, 'I think one is more than enough, don't you, when that one is Xavier Grey?'

'Now why do I feel that is an insult rather than a compliment?' Xavier drawled silkily. 'But no matter; one day you'll appreciate my finer qualities.'

And with that he shut the door.

CHAPTER EIGHT

ESSIE had a wonderful dinner and Xavier didn't put a foot wrong all night. He was polite and circumspect; even when he walked her to her car when the evening was over, he was studiously correct, merely touching her brow with his lips in a fleeting caress.

She didn't quite know why she had to stop the car halfway home and have a good cry, but she felt better when she had, and once she got home she took two aspirin with a glass of milk and went straight to sleep, physically, mentally and emotionally exhausted.

She got up with the sun the next morning, taking a cup of coffee into the garden with her as she sat on the wooden bench beneath a blue sky flecked with cotton-wool clouds and listened to the blackbird bossing about a group of starlings who had wandered into his holly tree.

Xavier wanted her to run the practice, with Jamie and at least one more vet—possibly two—assisting her, and she had said yes. She just hoped that was the right decision. She leant back against the bench as her mind reflected on all that had been said the night before.

She would still live here, with the new vet installed in the two rooms above the garages and a new office girl on a nine-to-five basis, and Marion would continue in Reception— nothing much had changed, Xavier had assured her coolly. But he needed someone who knew what they were doing, regarding the practice, and who was prepared to manage it for him. And he thought she was ideal.

And Jamie? she had asked worriedly, once the shock of his wanting her to manage the practice had abated somewhat. Did Jamie know what was being proposed? Because he had been working for Peter longer than she had, and she wouldn't want to upset him.

Xavier had stopped her at that point, his voice cool, as he had said yes, Jamie did know, and no, he wasn't upset. Jamie understood the practice was under new management and that his job was secure. From the tone of Xavier's voice at that point, Essie had rightly assumed that, as far as her new boss was concerned, he considered Jamie had every reason to be thankful.

'Peter's happy to spend the next few weeks until he leaves filling you in on anything and everything,' Xavier had said quietly, just as the waiter had brought their main course, 'but he thinks you're aware of most things anyway.'

Essie had nodded. In a small practice like theirs, it was necessary for each of them to be Jacks of all trades as well as master of the main one.

'And so you think you could handle the extra responsibility?' Xavier had asked quietly, his eyes intent on her lovely face. 'It wouldn't be too much for you?'

'Too much for me?' Her voice had been more astringent than was decorous for someone who had just been given a hefty rise in their salary and was talking to their new employer, and she'd tried to moderate it as she continued more sedately, 'Of course not.'

'I didn't think so.' And then he'd grinned at her and she'd lost all sense of time and place for a good thirty seconds.

Which brought her back to whether staying on at the practice was the right decision, Essie thought soberly, taking a great gulp of coffee and sighing loudly. Because Xavier would be around fairly often when he was in England.

But what else could she do? She finished the coffee and rose to her feet. She didn't want to lose her job and she certainly didn't want to lose her home. Perhaps it would all work out okay? They really could be just friends? The tumult of emotion inside her mocked the thought. Well, it would have to work, she thought determinedly as she walked back into the house. And this crazy desire for him that surged through her veins at the most inappropriate moments was a weakness she *would* get the victory over.

The next few months put paid to that thought ever becoming a reality, and by the beginning of October—and after a hot, sultry summer and manifold restless nights that had little to do with the weather and everything to do with Xavier—Essie was reconciled to the fact that Xavier Grey had been put on the earth to be a constant thorn in her side.

But shouldn't you want to get rid of a thorn? she asked herself as she sat checking the accounts in Peter's old office at the practice late one Saturday night. Certainly you shouldn't long for its appearance and dream about it at night!

And he had been so *different* since the new order of things had been established.

That he had taken her well and truly at her word was in no doubt. Every time he was at the flat—which was fairly frequently—he would take her out for a meal and then for a drive or to the theatre or cinema, ostensibly to talk about how the practice was running and discuss any practical hiccups, and the friend status was observed with frustrating good grace.

He made her laugh, he entertained her with anecdotes about his life, his work, Candy—anything important to him—and he encouraged her to talk with equal openness. It had got so she looked forward to him appearing, missed him when he wasn't around and—yes, *ached* to be with him, Essie admitted to herself morosely. And that was the last thing she'd planned on when she'd agreed to take on the responsibility for the practice.

Did he know? She shut her eyes tightly for a moment as she leant back in the big comfortable leather chair and rubbed her brow wearily. She hoped not. Oh, she did so hope not. She would die if he'd guessed she felt the way she did, especially after he could dismiss his desire for her with such apparent ease.

That he had a hectic and no doubt sexually active social life on both sides of the Atlantic she did not doubt, and she lived in dread that he would turn up at the flat one day with the female of the moment in tow.

But that was entirely his own business, of course. Her eyes snapped open as her mouth thinned into a determined line, and she attacked the list of figures in front of her with renewed vigour. But it was no good. Tonight she was tired in body and soul and she couldn't concentrate.

'Essie?' She hadn't heard the door to the office open and her face was startled as she glanced up to see Quinn—Peter's replacement—in the doorway. 'I've just made a list of the medication we need more of; you want it in here? And there's a pot of coffee brewing, if you're interested.'

'Yes and yes.' She grinned back into the dark, good-looking face, wondering, for the umpteenth time since Quinn had joined them, why she couldn't fancy him instead of Xavier. She knew he liked her in that way, and since she had got to know the handsome, dark-eyed Londoner, who was cool and self-controlled as well as good company, she'd often thought that if she was ever going to make a commitment to a man with a view to marriage and children Quinn would be the sort of man she could fall for.

But—something was missing. She liked Quinn, she liked him very much, and certainly since he'd been at the practice the number of women bringing their pets to the surgery had increased tenfold, but he didn't affect her like Xavier. She was in the minority here, she knew. Quinn had caused quite a stir roundabouts and he had something of an air of mystery about him, too, which the resident maidens found irresistible—but Xavier seemed to have made her immune to other men.

Not that she wanted marriage to anyone. She nodded at the thought as she rose and followed Quinn into the kitchen, where the delicious aroma of percolating coffee was scenting the air.

But if she *was* going to take the plunge a nice safe, comfortable existence working in the community with a fellow vet who understood the ups and downs of a veterinary life would be a definite asset. For sure. No playing hard and fast, no philandering and flitting from one woman to another—that could only be good, couldn't it?

Essie was still sitting in the kitchen some ten minutes later when, in the middle of Quinn relating an amusing incident at one of the farms between himself and an enormous and very bad-tempered old sow—which had Essie collapsed in gales of laughter—a deep, distinct and very cold voice from the kitchen doorway brought both their heads jerking round.

'Xavier, we didn't hear you,' Essie said, a trifle breathlessly, as the sight of him filled her vision and caused every nerve to tighten. He was wearing a long grey overcoat over his suit which increased the brooding, dark quality of his lethal attractiveness, and the silver gaze was narrowed on the pair of them with lazer-sharp intentness.

'Obviously.' It was drawled casually and accompanied by a lazy smile, but Essie got the impression Xavier was annoyed about something and this feeling was further heightened when he eyed Quinn with metallic stoniness and said, 'Working late, Quinn?'

'Quinn has been checking the medical cupboard and the stores and I was working on the accounts—' Essie stopped abruptly. Hang on, why was she almost apologising for the fact that they had been doing their jobs? she asked herself silently.

From the day he had started Quinn had never clock-watched or been chary about putting in as many extra hours as the job demanded. He was a tremendous asset to the practice—more so than Jamie, if she were being honest. Jamie—although an excellent vet—was hopeless regarding practical administrations and always eager to get away at the end of the day to see his girlfriend.

Her thoughts stiffened Essie's back and brought her small chin jutting—something the silver-blue gaze didn't miss—and when she said, her voice cool now, 'Do you want something, Xavier?' he surveyed her for some twenty seconds without replying, a perusal she returned without blinking.

'Yes.' He turned as he spoke and his voice was curt as he said over his shoulder, 'Come and see me before you leave, please, Essie.'

The easy, light atmosphere had been swept away by the force of Xavier's dark personality, and Quinn said, 'Shouldn't you go and see what he wants?'

Essie's voice was a quick snap as she answered, 'He can wait until I've finished my coffee.'

'Fine, fine.' Quinn raised his hands as he conceded to her tone, his ebony eyes smiling at her, and after catching sight of the perceptive and very astute expression on his handsome face, Essie gave a rueful smile of her own. Quinn didn't say much but he observed a great deal.

'Sorry.' She rubbed her nose irritably. 'But he makes me so *mad* at times.'

Yes, he'd noticed that, and he'd also noticed the way she came alive every time Xavier walked into a room; but, knowing Essie as he did, he couldn't visualise how all this was going to end. She would never be content to be a rich man's plaything, and Xavier Grey was a law unto himself. He just hoped she wasn't going to be hurt too badly.

It was another ten minutes before Essie walked up the stairs and knocked once on Xavier's front door. Right from the day Xavier had moved in she had avoided visiting the apartment, normally contriving that he came to

see her downstairs with any queries about the
practice and refusing any offers of coffee at
his place after their evenings out. To date, she
had only been in Peter's old home twice. But
she had noticed then that it was a totally different place from the family home Peter and
Carol had created. Noticed? She had never
been so overwhelmed in her life!

All the carpets had been ripped up and replaced with a deep-pile silvery-grey one which
she understood ran into every room. The enormous sitting room—Xavier had had one of the
walls knocked down to increase the space in
the living area—had linen wallpaper of a
deeper hue than the carpet, dramatic and undoubtedly expensive paintings on the walls,
and the suite was of charcoal leather. The hi-
fi was the latest state-of-the-art digital tech-
nology, and the TV posed as a small cinema,
occupying one corner of the room.

Altogether, it was a relentlessly masculine
apartment and aggressively luxurious.

'Ah, Essie.' Xavier opened the door just as
her hand was lifting to knock again and for a
moment she just stared at him, transfixed. 'I
was in the middle of having a shower, but
come in,' he said easily, waving his hand at

the room beyond as he stood aside for her to enter.

Essie forced herself to walk inside the flat because there was nothing else she could do, but she was finding it difficult to put one foot in front of the other.

Xavier had a towel wrapped low around his lean hips and he was wearing nothing else— *nothing*. She took a deep, silent and desperate pull of air before she turned to face him again.

His wet hair was hanging down over his forehead in small curls, his thickly muscled torso was tanned a golden brown and the crisp black hair on his chest was glistening with tiny droplets of water from the shower she had interrupted. His arms and legs and thighs looked hard and powerful and uncompromisingly masculine, and his virile maleness was flagrant.

It was, it was flagrant, she told herself silently, wanting to swallow and ease her suddenly dry throat but afraid she would gulp like a nervous child.

'You wanted a word?' She didn't know how the words came out so cool and steady but all she could put it down to was the composure born of acute shock.

Xavier nodded, indicating the leather sofa with another wave of his hand. 'Sit down,' he said casually, for all the world as though she were a normal guest he'd invited round for the evening, instead of his employee who was seeing him stark naked—or almost stark naked, Essie reflected helplessly. And that towel didn't look too secure, either; she just prayed it was more dependable than it looked.

'Thank you.' She sat down carefully, her knees tightly pressed together and her hands clasped primly in her lap. She had never felt so uncomfortable in her life.

'Drink?' He hadn't moved an inch; he just stood there watching her. 'You've had a coffee downstairs—how about a brandy to follow?' he invited lazily, his eyes glittering.

'No, thank you. I've got to drive home in a little while.'

'One brandy won't hurt,' he said soothingly, as though she were a small child he was having to reassure.

Oh, why couldn't he go and put some clothes on? A dressing gown. Anything! Every time she glanced his way, there appeared what seemed like acres and acres of bare flesh and she didn't know where to focus her gaze. 'No, really.' She trained her eyes on a point just past his left ear and managed to force a bright, interested note into her voice as she said, 'That's a lovely painting on the far wall.'

'Which one?' He turned to follow her glance and the towel tightened ominously over lean thighs.

Keep talking, Essie. Act naturally. 'The one with the splashes of orange and scarlet in the background.'

'The Grand Canyon at sunset.' He dismissed the beautiful abstract painting which had cost a small fortune with a total lack of interest. 'You're sure you don't want a brandy? Glass of wine? Soft drink?' he asked softly.

She shook her head quickly.

'Mind if I have one?'

'Of course not.'

Her breathing was uneven and shallow as he walked across to the cocktail cabinet to one side of the angelica-green raw silk drapes at the window and poured himself a stiff brandy.

He was lithe and fit and there didn't look to be an ounce of superfluous flesh anywhere on the hard, muscular body, but it was the touch of boyishness in the damp curls about his forehead that caught at Essie's heartstrings as he strolled across to face her again, and increased the dangerous magnetism he exuded as naturally as breathing a hundredfold.

'So…' He perched on the arm of one of the chairs and took a long swallow of the brandy as he surveyed her with narrowed eyes. 'How are things going?'

'Fine, fine.' He hadn't asked her to come up just to say that, had he?

'And Quinn? He's settled in well?' Xavier asked smoothly. He had left the interviews and hiring to her.

'Yes, he's great.' Essie thought of the hundred and one ways Quinn had contributed to the easy running of the practice in the three months he had been with them and her voice was warm. 'I don't know what we'd have done without him.'

'Is that so?'

'And, as you'll see from the figures this month, I think we can consider employing a veterinary nurse in the next little while. We need one desperately and of course they wouldn't be so expensive as a vet…' Essie's voice trailed away. He was looking at her very strangely. 'What's the matter?' she asked after a long, taut pause.

'Are you sleeping with Quinn?' Xavier asked almost conversationally, without moving a muscle.

'What?' She stared at him, totally taken aback and unsure if she had heard him properly. He couldn't have said what she thought he had just said, she told herself—and especially not in that even, expressionless voice.

'I said, are you sleeping with Quinn?' This time the cutting edge showed through. 'It's a simple enough question.'

'How dare you?' All the colour had drained from her face. 'How *dare* you suggest that?'

'I'm not suggesting, I'm asking,' Xavier said silkily.

'Well, you've got no right to ask,' she shot back furiously.

'I disagree.' He eyed her coolly. 'Emotional entanglements at work are always messy and invariably end in tears, and then there's the old scenario of one person leaving and so on. This is a nice little team, here; it'd be a shame to spoil it.'

And that was the only reason he was asking—because of his precious practice? Essie didn't know how to contain herself. He was the coldest, most inhuman, callous, *insensitive* pig of a man she had ever had the misfortune to meet!

She glared at him, her eyes shooting blue arrows directed straight at his unfeeling heart. 'And if I say yes, what are you going to do about it?' she asked with frigid dignity. 'Sack me, or him, or both of us?'

'Don't play with me, Essie.' For such a big man he moved like greased lightning and he had taken hold of her wrist and yanked her up out of the seat before she could blink. *'Are you sleeping with him?'*

'Let go of me!'

Immediately he had grabbed her, Xavier had realised his mistake—the memory of that other time when she had been so scared there in front of his eyes—and he had released her even before she had finished speaking. 'I'm sorry.' He took a step backwards as he spoke, feeling like the worst heel on earth as he saw the fear in her face. 'I'm sorry, Essie. It's all right. I wouldn't harm a hair of your head.'

She stared at him, speechless and swaying slightly, but she could see he was as horrified by developments as she was, and something in his stricken expression—which was so at variance with the cool, calm ice-man that was

Xavier Grey—helped her regain her equilib-
rium enough to say, 'I know that.'

And she did. She didn't ask herself how she
had come by the knowledge, but she knew he
wouldn't resort to physical violence with a
woman, whatever the provocation.

Xavier drained the last of his brandy in one
gulp before saying thickly, 'I need another of
these,' and brushing past her towards the cocktail cabinet.

He was halfway across the sitting room
when she said, 'I am not sleeping with Quinn,
as it happens; there is nothing of that nature
between us. Believe it or not, we really are just
good friends.' Her voice was low but firm.

He didn't halt in his stride but she saw her
words register in the stiffening of his back and,
after he had poured himself another drink, he
drank at least half of it before turning to face
her. 'He fancies you, you know that, don't
you?'

Essie didn't prevaricate. She was still standing where he had jerked her and she looked at
him proudly. 'We're working colleagues, like
I said, Xavier, and Quinn is too professional
to complicate things. Besides, you know my

views on involvement. My work and career are the only important things to me.'

'That's a hell of a loss to the male sex.' He approached her slowly, his eyes never leaving hers.

She tried to smile, to take the comment as the light compliment she was sure it was, but she couldn't. She just watched him approach— all six-foot-plus, lean, dark, dangerous masculinity and hard control—and waited for him to reach her.

'You're very beautiful, Essie. Inside and out.' He lifted her chin to meet his eyes and his gaze locked on hers. 'I'm crazy about you, you know that, don't you?' he said gruffly.

'Xavier, don't.'

'I have to.' He bent his head and kissed her, and the warm, honey-sweet sensations she remembered from the last time she had been in his arms trickled into her bloodstream. 'I've been patient, haven't I?' he said with a wry, almost bewildered note in his voice, as though patience was not something he was familiar with.

'Xavier, I never lied to you, you know that. I made it clear—'

'Crystal-clear,' he agreed softly.

Why did he have to do this now, with his broad-shouldered, lean-hipped magnificence indisputably blatant and so seductively at odds with the little-boy appeal of those stray damp curls on his forehead and the tenderness in his aggressively attractive face?

'So you know exactly how things are,' Essie said desperately.

'Exactly.'

He put his mouth to hers again and she trembled at the contact, and immediately the kiss deepened, feeding the weakening excitement that was curling through her limbs.

He pulled her against him and she shivered as the scent of clean, fresh male skin enveloped her, her hands curled against the solid wall of his chest where crisp body hair caused her fingers to tighten.

His mouth was erotic and searching and his body was hard and determined to stamp her softness with the knowledge of his maleness, his hands moving over her back and waist in a steady, languorous rhythm that moved her against him and fed his desire.

Her body had come alive—she could feel every feminine part of her opening like a tender bud before the heat of the sun—and it was exhilarating, thrilling—and dangerous. *Dangerous.*

She tried to pull away, but he wasn't ready to let her go yet. After one brief protest, she melted against him again, swollen and moist.

Xavier was breathing hard, his body rigid and his heart pounding like a drum beneath the veneer of golden skin, and she could feel the control he was exercising. He was exploring her mouth, his tongue hot and sweet as it fuelled the drugging passion racing through her veins, and she moaned softly, hardly able to believe the way she was feeling.

'Sweet, sweet Essie.' He had wrenched his mouth from hers and now his voice was uneven but tender as he put the brake on their caresses. As she looked up at him, a question mark in her eyes, he said more roughly, 'A few moments more and I shan't be able to stop. You understand me?'

Yes, she understood, but such was her desire that she had to clench her teeth against the urge to fall against him again in total surrender.

'Essie, there are things I have to say to you, things you have to understand, but now is not the time,' Xavier said thickly. She was still standing so close she could feel the stirrings of his body and now her cheeks were flushed and hot at the hard, alien power beneath the towel.

'I need to talk to you and it can't wait, not if I want to remain sane,' he said with a touch of dark humour. 'You're coming out for a drive with me tomorrow, and we'll call in for lunch somewhere.'

It was an order, not an invitation, and normally Essie would have rebelled at the autocratic tone, but she was unable to string two words together right at that moment. She nodded, backing away from him without speaking, and he stood watching her until she reached the doorway, his muscled frame perfectly still and his eyes two slits of burning light in the darkness of his face.

'I'll pick you up at ten.'

She nodded again before she turned into the hall and then she had reached the front door and was out onto the landing, her legs shaking and her head whirling as she fairly flew down the stairs and into the office to fetch her bag and keys.

She could see the lights from Quinn's tiny home above the garages as she left but little was registering beyond a dizzying spiral of apprehension regarding the next day.

She must have been crazy, *crazy*, to agree to go out with him when it was obvious what he wanted to say. It was going to be the no-holds-barred, cards-on-the-table proposition she now saw he had been intending all along. The last few months—his apparent lack of interest in her as anything but a friend and the steady chipping away at the barriers she had put up against him at first—had all been for one purpose. To get her into his bed.

He was a ruthless but brilliant strategist, she thought soberly as she drove carefully home, aware she had to be extra vigilant on the dark country roads, given the way she was feeling. He had played it all perfectly, right down to what she now saw were his suspicions regarding Quinn. He had thought she'd given Quinn what she was withholding from him—that was what had made him so mad—but, as usual, he had turned her emotions upside down until he had got her to admit what he needed to know. And then he had proved very succinctly that, despite all her fine words, when he clicked his fingers she jumped.

She gripped the steering wheel so tightly, her knuckles shone white.

He had shown her yet again she was putty in his hands, but if he thought he was going to win he could think again. However much she loved him, they could have no future.

Loved him?

For a moment she thought the tree had jumped into her path, until she realised she had swerved involuntarily and missed it by a hair's breadth.

She brought the car to a shuddering halt, her face chalk-white and her eyes wide and staring. She did love him. She had loved him for months. He had eased himself into her life, taking over her thought processes, her mind, her heart, with calculated persistence. He had played a cunning tactical game and he had won.

He had seduced her. Oh, not in a crude physical sense, but in every other way he had manoeuvred himself into the very fibre of her life, her being, and that was much, much worse than merely taking her body.

She sat bent over the steering wheel, her head spinning. And now he was going to go for the grand slam tomorrow. He had told her he wanted her complete and utter capitulation, that he wouldn't take her in the heat of the moment without being sure she knew exactly what she was doing and wasn't being swept away by momentary passion, and he had obviously judged the time was now right.

With his vast knowledge of women, he had clearly been observing her, watching out for all the signs, and she must have given herself away.

She groaned, shaking her head at her own gross stupidity. She had thought Colin was a control freak—Andrew, too, in a different, less physical way—but Xavier put both of them into the shade. She wanted to hate him—more than anything on earth she wanted to hate him—but she didn't. She couldn't.

The minutes ticked by in the cool of the October night, the chilly autumn wind outside the car moaning softly as it disturbed the leaves on the row of giant oak trees that bordered both sides of the road.

It was nearly half an hour later, and after Essie was chilled to the bone, that she raised her head. Her eyes were burningly dry.

She would keep the lunch date with Xavier tomorrow. She stared into the shadows beyond the windscreen. And when he propositioned her—as he was sure to—she would be ready for him. She had imagined herself living in this little part of the world for the rest of her life, but it looked as though it wasn't to be.

A sharp pain sliced through her heart and the hot tears shot against the back of her eyelids, but she blinked them away determinedly.

She would probably have to leave her little cottage, move far away and begin again, but she could do it. She could. Even in the unlikely event of a job opportunity in the surrounding area, she couldn't take the risk of ever meeting Xavier when he was visiting the flat. This had to be a clean break— a once-and-for-all severing of any likelihood of further contact. There was no other way she could survive the pain of what she had to do.

CHAPTER NINE

ESSIE had a tormented night but the morning saw her pale and determined.

She spent much longer than usual on her make-up as the ravages of an agonising sleepless night took some time to hide. But by the time she had finished—her slender body clothed in a bright scarlet sweater and black trousers and boots, and her mass of golden curls tied high on the back of her head with a scarlet ribbon—no one could have guessed that her heart was breaking.

Certainly to Xavier—as he watched her leave the cottage at ten sharp, in answer to the toot of the Mercedes's horn—Essie looked the epitome of bright colour-filled days and romantic nights, her delicate beauty overwhelming.

'Hi.' His voice was deep and husky as she brushed past him and slid into the passenger seat of the car.

'Hello.' Her voice was restrained but he could understand that, he told himself silently as he shut the car door and walked round the bonnet to the driving seat. She must be wondering what the hell this was all about. But he couldn't go on like this another day—last night had told him that, if nothing else.

'I'm sorry to drag you out of bed so early on your day off.' His eyes were soft as he slid into the driving seat, but she stared straight ahead without glancing at him.

'That's okay.' She shrugged offhandedly. 'I never stay in bed late in the mornings, anyway.'

You would if you were mine. In fact, the bedroom would take on a whole new connotation for both of us.

He pictured his bedroom in his house in Canada as he started the engine. He had designed it himself, and the wide expanse of varnished wood floor led to a huge sunken bed that dominated the massive room, the walk-in wardrobes and bookcase and hi-fi and TV just window-dressing for the enormous round billowy bed that measured over eight feet in diameter.

He could see her in that bed nestled amongst the pillows and cushions as he pampered and pleased her. The erotic fantasy was causing problems with a certain part of his anatomy, and he found he had to carefully adjust his position in his seat as he drove the big car up the narrow lane away from the cottage.

They drove in silence for some miles—Xavier because he was still having difficulty mastering his imagination with the sweet fragrance of her teasing his nostrils, and Essie because she was as wound up as a coiled spring—but after a few minutes he turned to her. 'This is your patch; anywhere in particular you'd like to go?'

She shrugged again. 'Anywhere. I don't mind.'

This time the tightness in her voice got through to him and he glanced at her more intently, the warm light that had turned the silver-blue gaze liquid beginning to die.

'What's the matter?' he asked quietly. 'If it's about last night, that wasn't intentional, believe it or not. I came down here this weekend intending to speak to you, not seduce you.'

She did glance at him then. He had sounded as though he meant it, but almost immediately cold logic stepped in. Of course he was going to say that, she told herself caustically. What else could he say—I've been waiting until I thought you were ripe for the having, and last night convinced me this was the weekend I get lucky?

'Really.' Her voice was cold.

'Yes, really,' he answered, somewhat tersely. 'Look, I can't say what I have to say driving this damn car. Is there a park somewhere near here where we could sit for a while?'

Oh, what was she going to do? What was she going to *do*? What she had to do. The answer was there—it had been all the time.

'Turn left at the next junction.' She continued to direct him until they turned into the gates of the nature reserve and picnic area that was always chock-a-block full of screaming children and harassed parents in the summer, but which was deserted today, except for the resident ducks and swans on the cold, silent lake.

He cut the engine immediately, turning to her in one sharp motion as he said, 'Essie, look at me.'

And she did, aware he would never know the willpower it took.

'There's no right way to say this and it's probably not the right time, either, but I'm going to go stark staring crazy if I don't get it off my chest.'

Here it comes. Essie was conscious of thinking that his eyes held the brilliant luminescence of pure mother-of-pearl as she stared at him, and that he had never looked so handsome.

'I love you. I want you to be my wife.'

He heard her shocked indrawn breath and saw the way her pupils enlarged until the blue was almost swallowed up by black. 'You don't mean it.'

It was a faint whisper but it caused his eyes to narrow as he said, very calmly, 'The hell I don't.' So—he hadn't expected her to fall on his neck, had he? Xavier asked himself with rigid control. He knew that there was still a long way to go but damn it—she *had* grown to like him a bit over the last months. And the mutual physical attraction between them was so strong he could taste it, the minute their eyes met.

'You...you said that you've had a lot of women and that you don't like to get involved. You *said,*' she mumbled accusingly.

'I have and I didn't,' he said imperturbably. 'And then I met you.'

She was wringing her hands in her lap and now he reached over and took them in his own, his voice soft and deep. 'Essie, I know you still have things to work through and I don't want to rush you,' he said softly, willing himself to keep his voice and his emotions under control. 'But I need to know...I need to have some sort of idea whether there is any hope or not. I want you—I want you in every way it's possible for a man to want a woman, and I want it for life.'

'No. *No.*' She had never known such fear. If anyone had told her just a few hours ago that Xavier would say he loved her, that he wanted to *marry* her, she would have said it would make her the happiest woman on earth. And she would have thought she meant it.

But love meant commitment—total commitment, and marriage... She had seen what marriage did to a woman when she thought she was in love. And how did you know what love was, anyway? Her mother had been sexually attracted to Colin—she had told Essie so one day, after they had both endured a particularly vicious beating and Essie had screamed at her mother, demanding to know the reason she had married Colin in the first place. She had mistaken sexual attraction for love, her mother had told her, her bruised face awash with tears. And he had been so gentle, so kind, so loving before they had tied the knot. He had been a different man…

'I won't accept no.' He had seen the wash of emotion over her face and it had made his stomach curdle. 'Whatever's happened in the past, we can work through this. I can make you love me, Essie.'

She jerked her head back away from him, the deep scarlet of the jumper accentuating the paleness of her face. 'No,' she said again, her voice stony.

'Yes.' Xavier drew in a deep, hard breath. 'I know what it's like to go through the mill— hell, at one time I thought my family had the monopoly on the concept, until I learnt there are hundreds of different ways for people to get hurt. Since I met you I've done a lot of hard thinking. I admit, at the beginning, I was attracted to you—physically, I mean—and that I had the idea I could woo you into my bed. But this is more than that.'

'You're saying that because we haven't gone to bed yet.'

'Is that what he did, Essie? Took you to bed and then used and hurt you? For crying out loud, tell me,' Xavier said grimly.

He loved her. *He loved her.* Did she believe that? Essie asked herself silently. Yes, she did. As far as she could be sure of anyone, that was. But her mother had been an intelligent and warm human being and she had been sure Colin loved her, too. And that might even have been true. But then they had got married and life had turned into an unmitigated nightmare.

Perhaps Xavier wouldn't hurt her—physically, that was. In fact, she was sure he wouldn't. But if she married him she would become more vulnerable than she could bear to imagine. Because one thing was for sure in all this—she loved him. And that gave him a power over her that was unthinkable. She didn't dare to take such a chance. She just didn't dare.

'You talk about him, but there wasn't a him—at least, not in the sense you mean,' she began quietly, her voice flat and terribly controlled. 'But I'll tell you, if it helps you to understand why there can never be anything between us, why I'd never be any good as a wife.'

She told him it all. The desolation when her beloved father had died; the excitement when her mother had met Colin and she had acquired two future stepsisters and a stepbrother to play with. And then the marriage, and the despair and misery that had followed. The beatings, the cruelty. And then how she had gone to university, heartsore and craving love, tenderness, protection. And she'd met Andrew.

Xavier listened, forcing himself to remain silent as she poured it all out but feeling as sick as a dog.

'I know where I am with my work, Xavier.' Her voice was dead-sounding as she finished. 'And I'm good at what I do. I can control my life. It's up to me how many hours I work and when I take my holidays. I can decide to sleep in late on my days off or be up at six in the morning in the garden—'

'I'm talking about marriage, for crying out loud, not pruning the roses.' He had spoken out of his frustration and impotent rage at the two men who had damaged her so severely, but almost immediately he took hold of himself. He was fighting for everything he had ever wanted, here; he couldn't afford to give in to any destructive emotion.

'Essie, just listen to me a minute, would you, without saying anything?' he asked softly.

She nodded, but her eyes were as wary as a wounded doe's. She tried to remove her hands from his, but he wouldn't let her.

'My childhood—well, you know about my childhood,' he said abruptly, taking a deep breath before he spoke again. 'I grew up without a father and Natalie was, to all intents and purposes, my mother. It wasn't the greatest model of family life for any kid, and some of the men who used to visit my mother were supposedly happily married, but they were game for an affair when they thought they could get away with it. It soured me, Essie.'

He paused. 'And then Candy was born and Natalie died, and for the next few years, until she died, my mother tried to make atonement, believing Natalie's death was her fault. I believed it was her fault, too. I still do,' he added grimly. 'But, whatever, we brought up Candy between us until the responsibility became fully mine, and I embraced it gladly. I look on her as a daughter, not a niece, and until I met you I thought she was the only family I would ever have—all I wanted, I guess. I didn't want to get involved in any more human tragedies;

living life on my own terms meant everything
to me.'

He meant every word, she could see that,
and it made all this a hundred times—a thousand times—worse. He had the courage to
reach out, to still *believe*, but she didn't. She
just didn't, Essie thought numbly. Oh, why had
he told her he loved her? Why had he had to
go and say that?

'All that's happened to you, Essie, I understand. I do understand, but you can't let those
men—both shallow, stunted human beings in
their different ways—ruin your life. Don't you
see? We've got something good between us.
It's been there since that very first ridiculous
moment when you were tottering up the aisle
after Christine and I thought you were suffer-
ing from the effects of the night before. I
wanted you then. Badly.'

'That's lust. You didn't know me,' she said
stonily.

'I know you now and it isn't lust.' He
paused. 'Well, that's not strictly true. I do lust
after you. I adore you; I eat, sleep and breathe
you. But I love you, most of all.'

What had it taken a cold, hard man like
Xavier to admit all this? Essie thought desper-

ately. To come to terms with being vulnerable for the first time in his adult life?

She didn't want to hurt him—the last thing in all the world she wanted to do was to hurt him—but she had to do this. It would be better for both of them in the long run. But her heart was feeling as though it was being wrenched out by the roots and never had she felt so awful, so cruel.

'Xavier, I don't want what you want.' She lifted her head which had been drooping down and looked him full in the face. 'You have to accept that, please. I don't want to love anyone and I don't want to get married.'

'I don't believe that.'

'It's the truth.'

The sky was clouding over, a deep dove-grey replacing the patches of blue of early morning, and just in front of them a pair of swans suddenly rose into the air, their somewhat ungainly take-off negated by the pure beauty of their airborne flight. The sombre light, the darkening grey sky and the virgin purity of the snow-white birds caused a lump in Essie's throat as a poignancy so painful as to be unbearable gripped her. She would remember this moment for ever, she told herself with agonising clarity.

'You care about me.' Xavier hadn't got to where he was by admitting defeat and he wasn't about to give in now. 'And sexually we would be perfect; take it from one who knows. Whatever you shared with Andrew would be better with me.'

'I didn't sleep with Andrew.' She pulled her hands free now, brushing a weary hand across her forehead as she forced herself to say, 'And I couldn't sleep with anyone I didn't love.'

'I'll make you love me.'

Oh, my love, my love, if you only knew. Essie steeled herself to lie, just wanting it all to end now.

'I've never slept with anyone, Xavier, and I don't *want* to,' she said unflinchingly. 'I don't love you and I don't want to love you. I want to run my life on my own terms, like you have. I don't *want* to change. I can't change and I won't.'

'I don't believe you,' he said again.

But she could see from the stricken look in the silver-blue eyes that he did. 'You want me, Essie, sexually, and that's a start,' he said torturedly, fighting to the last breath as he pulled her into him, careless of the controls of the car, and took her lips in a kiss that spoke of savage frustration.

She didn't try to fight him. She didn't move at all; she simply made herself remain still and unresponsive beneath the fevered embrace—and that was the hardest thing of all. He would never understand that it was her very love for him that was stopping them ever coming together, that the way she felt gave him the sort of power she could never willingly entrust to any man. And if she couldn't trust him, if she couldn't give him the unconditional faith and love that was the foundation of any relationship, she would end up destroying them both.

And she couldn't. Even now, after all he'd said, she had to be honest with herself and admit she couldn't. He was too charismatic, too attractive, too strong and sure of himself. How could a man like that ever be satisfied with someone like her, with all her hang-ups and insecurities and fears? she asked herself, fighting with all of her strength the rising desire that had her melting inside.

When he finally raised his head, the look on his face smote her heart. 'I'll take you home,' he said dully, starting the engine as he spoke.

'Xavier, you'll meet someone else and—'

'Don't!' It was so savage she recoiled from him as if he'd struck her. 'Don't say another word, Essie.'

And she didn't. All through the drive home, as the rain began to pelt in gusts against the windscreen and the wind caused the branches of the trees to moan and writhe, Essie sat huddled in the corner of her seat, her face white and her hands clenched in her lap.

When the Mercedes pulled to a halt in the small parking place outside the cottage, Xavier was out of his seat like a shot, opening her door for her with a stony face and giving a curt nod in answer to her agonised, 'Thank you.'

He had climbed back in the car before she had opened the front door but didn't start the engine until she was inside the cottage—courteous to the last, she thought painfully. And then he was gone, not in a screech of brakes or a blur of metal as she might have expected, but slowly, deliberately.

His measured exit was more final than any words could have expressed.

CHAPTER TEN

Just how final Xavier's departure had been, Essie didn't fully realise until the next morning.

She had slept very little the night before, in spite of the previous sleepless night, and after rising at five and forcing some toast and coffee past the huge lump in her throat she was at the practice by seven, dreading the possibility she might see Xavier before he left but longing for it too. She was a mess—a total emotional mess, she admitted desperately.

The change in the weather from the mild dry weeks they had been enjoying before the weekend hadn't abated—it was a good few degrees colder today and the wind and rain seemed to have set in. But it suited her desolation. She couldn't have coped with bright sunshine and blue skies. She didn't deserve them, either. She was a coward, a total and absolute coward, she told herself bitterly as she opened the front door of the practice and stepped into the cold hall—the central heating didn't switch on until seven-thirty and the old house was draughty. But even knowing she was a coward hadn't changed her mind.

The Mercedes hadn't been parked at the front of the house as she had expected, and now Essie walked through to the back door and peered out into the clients' car park which, apart from Quinn's very nice Aston Martin sitting quietly in one corner, was empty.

He must have left very early. Her stomach lurched and she bit down hard on her lower lip. And she had no idea when he would be back, although she would have to get in contact with him within the next few days to give her notice and find out what he wanted to do about replacing her.

And then that last thought was taken care of when she walked into the office, carrying the mug of coffee she had just made and which almost ended up all over the desk as she caught sight of the envelope with her name on it, written in that familiar strong black scrawl.

She sat down before she opened it—her legs felt distinctly wobbly—and then took several gulps of coffee as she stared at the expensive-looking envelope with the monogram 'XG' in gold in the top left-hand corner.

'Come on, Essie. If you had the strength to send him away, you've got the strength to open this flipping envelope.' Her voice sounded hollow and very small and, with an exclamation of exasperation, she leant forward, picking up the envelope and opening it carefully as though it were going to bite her.

It didn't. It did far, far worse than that. Xavier had written:

I'm leaving tonight, Essie, and I shan't be back. I don't want you to lose your job or your home because of my mistake—

Mistake: he thought falling in love with her had been a mistake, Essie thought rawly as pain swamped her.

—and to that end I'm making the house and the practice over to you. It will be legal, no strings attached, and I would prefer all contact to be through our solicitors. Don't say you can't accept it—this place means everything to you and it won't even make a dent in my bank balance. The last few months have shown me you have a good head for business as well as a heart for your work, and with no mortgage hanging over your head you will make this into exactly what you want it to be. Good luck and God bless. X.

How long Essie sat there with the tears streaming down her face and her heart in pieces she didn't know, but when Quinn popped his head round the door the panic and concern in his voice as he spoke her name lifted her head.

'What is it?' He had reached her side in a moment, his good-looking face creased with concern, and when Jamie followed some minutes later and Essie was still crying Quinn gestured towards the telephone. 'Call the doctor.'

'No.' Essie tried desperately to control herself. 'No, I'll be all right. It's just…'

'Just?'

Both men were kneeling in front of her now, one of her hands in each of theirs, and she shook her head weakly as she said, 'I've made the biggest mistake of my life.'

'It can't be that bad. What is it? A wrong diagnosis?' Jamie asked before Quinn nudged him quiet.

She stared helplessly at them both, the tears threatening to well again as their kindness touched her, and in answer she removed her hands from theirs and picked up the letter from the desk, passing it to them without a word.

She watched their eyes skim the few lincs and when their gazes lifted to her face she said brokenly, 'He asked me to marry him. He's in love with me.'

'And you?' Quinn asked quietly. 'Do you love him?'

She stared at them for a moment and then nodded slowly. 'But he doesn't know. I sent him away,' she mumbled thickly. 'I...I was scared—of love, commitment, all that.'

'So tell him.' Quinn spoke as if it were all very simple. 'If he really loves you he'll understand, and if this letter is anything to go by he does. So tell him what you've told us, Essie.'

'You don't understand.' She looked up at them both as they rose to their feet. 'The things I said yesterday—he'll never believe me now.'

'You don't know that for sure.' Jamie added his weight to Quinn's suggestion. 'And it's worth a try. What have you got to lose?'

Nothing. She had lost everything that would ever matter. The thought brought her shoulders slumping before she straightened them purposefully. That attitude wasn't the one that had got her through the years of cruelty at Colin's hands and then her mother's death, she told herself resolutely, and if she had let herself think like that at university, after Andrew's betrayal, she could have ended up in a psychiatric ward.

She would tell Xavier what she had learnt. That she had fallen in love with him; that she had loved him for weeks, months; that he'd opened up her understanding and shown her the past was the past and she had to go forward. With him. If he still wanted her, that was.

Even when she had rejected his unburdening of himself over his past, when she had been too wrapped up in herself and her own fears to respond to what she now saw was a tremendous step for him, he hadn't wanted revenge. He had simply given her what he saw as her heart's desire. This house and practice. He had given it to her—no strings attached.

Her throat constricted but she was determined she wasn't going to cry any more. She
had wasted enough time already.

Xavier's secretary was ice-cool and very professional, but she had a job to keep the irritation out of her voice as she said, 'Miss Russell,
this is the third call today and the answer is
the same as it was yesterday and the day before
that. Mr Grey cannot be disturbed.'

'When will he be available?'

'I've no idea.'

'Have you told him I've phoned?' Essie
asked doggedly.

'I record every call Mr Grey receives,' the
secretary said patiently, 'but you must understand he is an extremely busy man and divides
his time between here and Canada.'

'I really do need to speak with Mr Grey very
urgently.' Essie paused. This wasn't getting
her anywhere. 'So perhaps I'd better come
down to the office and camp out on the doorstep?' she suggested sweetly. 'Yes, I'll do that.
Perhaps you would let Mr Grey know I'll be
arriving some time tomorrow and I shall stay
around as long as it takes.'

The secretary raised her eyebrows at Xavier who was listening to the call and he shook his head, making a sharp cutting motion with his hand.

'That really wouldn't be a good idea, Miss Russell,' the clear, cold voice said evenly.

'On the contrary, I think it's an excellent idea.'

'You could be kept waiting for days and still end up disappointed.'

'I might be waiting for weeks but I assure you I shan't be disappointed, because I intend to see Mr Grey at the end of it,' Essie answered calmly.

'I'll take the call in my office.'

Xavier had growled at his secretary and now, as she spoke into the receiver, saying, 'Mr Grey has just arrived and can spare you two minutes, Miss Russell,' she was thinking, What on earth has this woman got that the rest of us haven't? She had never thought to see the day when a woman got under her illustrious boss's skin, but it had arrived—and how. He was normally all cool detachment and insouciant control when the affair was going on, and brisk indifference when he finished it, but this time... He'd been like a bear with a sore head for days now, snapping and snarling until everyone was tiptoeing about on eggshells.

'Hello, Essie.'

Essie's heart stopped beating and then made a determined effort to jump out of her chest as she heard Xavier's deep, faintly accented voice on the other end of the telephone.

'Hello.' She was breathless and it wouldn't do. She took a deep breath when all she really wanted to do was to burst into tears and wail her love for him over the line. 'I've been trying to talk to you the last few days,' she said with careful control, 'but I understand you've been very busy.'

'This is pointless, Essie.' In typical Xavier fashion, there was no beating about the bush or inane social niceties. 'Everything that needs to be arranged can be done through our solicitors and it will be easier that way for both of us.'

'Xavier, I can't possibly accept such a gift—'

'You can. It will be made over to you whether you want it or not, and then it's up to you what you decide to do with it,' Xavier said crisply. 'Now, if that's all, I have an important—'

'It's not all, it's not even the beginning,' Essie interrupted hotly, terrified he was going to put the phone down on her. 'I was wrong, stupid, all upset when we talked that morning,' she said feverishly, her words tumbling over each other in her agitation. 'I didn't mean it when I said I didn't love you. I do.'

There was a long, long silence and then Xavier said, his voice cool and very remote, 'I appreciated your honesty, Essie. Believe me. And I prefer it to the sort of misplaced gratitude you seem to be labouring under now.'

'It's not gratitude! Well, I am grateful—of course I am—but that's not why I'm saying I love you,' she protested somewhat incoherently. 'I'd been fighting it for weeks; I realise that now.'

'And when did this illuminating revelation occur?' Xavier asked sardonically. 'When you had had a chance to dwell on the sob story you heard and your soft woman's heart was stirred? Or perhaps when you felt such a sense of indebtedness that you were prodded into sacrificial mode?'

'No, it's not like that,' she said again. 'And it wasn't a sob story; I know that. You would never behave like that.'

'Essie, you don't know the first thing about me and we'll just keep it that way.'

Oh, this was awful—worse than she could have imagined. He had retreated into that formidable armour and she would never be able to get through to him. He thought she was feeling sorry for him and that her pity and sense of obligation at what he had done for her had prompted her to ring him.

'Xavier, listen to me. Please, please, listen—'

'No, Essie.' It was unequivocally final. 'Let's finish this with a little dignity on both sides. I had the presumption to think I could make you love me like I love you and I was wrong. This whole affair is my fault, totally my fault, and I understand that. We both know I bought the practice so I could be near you, and that doesn't apply any more. You're a good vet, and you've got a good team with Jamie and Quinn. You can build that practice up and make it work for all of you and that's good.'

She couldn't bear this. She pictured him in her mind's eye: the dark, chiselled face and lean, muscular body and, as though he were in front of her, she saw the naked agony in the silver eyes that had been there on that Sunday morning.

'It's not good, not without you here,' she tried helplessly.

'Goodbye, Essie.'

She stood for some moments with the receiver in her hand, unable to believe he had put the phone down.

He had really gone and she wasn't going to be able to get him back, and she wasn't talking about another phone call.

The next seven days felt like seven weeks, but at the end of them Essie knew she had finally grown up.

How could you go through all she had done in the past and not be grown-up? she asked herself as she sat staring at the documents her solicitor had sent to her that morning for signature, documents that signed over the house and the practice to her. But she hadn't been.

She had thought that self-protection was the pivot on which to build her life and her future, and she had been so wrapped up in her own hurts and disappointments that she had acted like a foolish, frightened child when Xavier had reached out to her with his love.

He was her only chance of happiness, the only future she wanted, and somehow she had to convince him of that. If he loved her even half as much as she loved him, he'd be in torment right now, and all the things that had gripped her in the past—her self-respect, her pride and self-esteem—counted as nothing compared to that.

But a phone call wouldn't work; she would have to go and see him. The prospect was daunting. She knew he had business interests in Dorking and Crawley, but his offices, along with his penthouse, were in London, and that was where she was most likely to catch him. And it wouldn't be any good ringing beforehand, either; surprise was the best weapon.

And if he wouldn't see her? She set her shoulders determinedly. She wouldn't take no for an answer. And if he wasn't there? Then she'd wait for him; she'd return day after day, if that was what it took.

Quinn and Jamie were wonderfully supportive when she told them what she was going to do, assuring her she had no need to worry about anything at the practice and they would cope however long she was away. She didn't tell them that the practice was the last thing on her mind—she didn't think it appropriate for the new owner to be so dispassionate about what had, until recently, been her all-consuming obsession—but it was further evidence of just how much she had changed in a few short days and it amazed her.

She arrived in London—courtesy of the early train—the next morning, just before nine o'clock. Just to be on the safe side, she had brought her overnight case with her. She had dressed very carefully for her visit to his offices, her smart jacket and pencil-slim skirt in midnight-blue both chic and feminine but businesslike, too. The last image she needed to portray was that of a bumbling hill-billy, she thought nervously as she stepped out of the taxi in front of the massive building wherein Grey Electronics was housed at exactly half-past nine.

By a quarter to ten she was drinking coffee with Xavier's secretary—who was *much* nicer than she sounded on the phone—and at eleven Quinn was shooting up to her in the Aston Martin with her passport on the front seat, and Essie was in possession of an air ticket to Canada on a flight leaving Heathrow later that day.

Candy had been involved in an accident—a *terrible* accident, Jade, Xavier's secretary, had told her somewhat tearfully on her arrival— and was fighting for her life in a hospital close to where they lived. It had happened three days ago and Xavier had taken the next plane out. He was devastated, absolutely devastated, but of course she could guess that.

Yes, she could guess that.

Oh, my love, my love—and you're facing it all alone, like you've had to face everything in life. The coals of fire were smouldering on her head.

Essie never could remember much of the long flight to Vancouver. It passed in a daze of faces and meals and social niceties that she endured because she had to. Every nerve, every cell in her body was crying out to Xavier.

If she hadn't been so stupid, if she had been brave enough to reach out to him when he had offered her heaven, he wouldn't have to be en- during this alone. She would have been at his side, supporting him, taking care of all the lit- tle things like making sure he was eating and sleeping enough. But then, he had never had anyone love him the way she was going to love him, she told herself stoutly when the self-recrimination threatened to overcome her. *And she was going to love him.* They would have to carry her away from him kicking and screaming, because it was the only way she was going to leave him.

And Candy. Poor, poor Candy. The russet-haired, blue-eyed young woman was there on the screen of her mind. Harper had been killed in the car accident that had put Candy in Intensive Care; how was Xavier going to break the news to her, if she came round from the coma she was in? She was twenty-three, he had been twenty-five—they had had all their lives before them. Oh, why couldn't this plane go faster? She needed to be at Xavier's side.

Essie was working on automatic when she walked out of the terminal, one hand clutching her overnight case and the other holding the address and the telephone numbers of both the hospital and Xavier's home.

Because of the time difference, the plane had landed at eight in the evening Canadian time, and the sunshine and low humidity the coast of British Columbia enjoyed all year round made the air cool and refreshing to Essie's jaded senses.

It was difficult to imagine a more lovely setting for a city than Vancouver—the ocean surrounded the city on three sides and the mountains seemed almost to rise out of the water, forming a rugged and majestic backcloth to the city—but for once Essie was oblivious to the beauty that would normally have thrilled her.

Her one, consuming desire was to get to Xavier's side—nothing else mattered—and she was virtually deaf and blind to the vibrant city as a cab sped her through cosmopolitan streets overlooked by the mighty Grouse Mountain.

She had decided to try the hospital first—purely on instinct—and so it was, at just after nine that evening, that she was shown into a waiting area by a friendly-faced nurse. 'I'll just go and have a word with Mr Grey,' the young woman said quietly, 'and let him know you're here.'

'He hasn't left yet, then?' Essie's heart had started to pound and her mouth was suddenly dry.

'No, not yet. He normally stays until gone midnight and then he's back at six or seven in the morning,' the nurse said ruefully. 'We're all expecting to have another patient on our hands if he doesn't get some rest. You say you're a friend who has just flown out from England?'

Essie took a deep breath. She had to see him and every bone in her body was telling her she had to catch him with his guard down—before that formidable mask slotted into place and the shield went up—and what was she going to say wasn't exactly a lie… 'I'm his fiancée,' she said firmly. 'He only asked me to marry him a couple of weeks before this happened; it's such a tragedy.'

The young woman nodded, her face sympathetic.

'Could I surprise him?' Essie asked softly. 'I'd really like to, if that's all right? He doesn't know I'm coming and I know he'll be thrilled to see me.' Okay, she was pushing the truth a little, but the situation demanded it.

'I don't know.' The nurse glanced around as if seeking advice from the air. 'His niece is in a coma, you understand, and Mr Grey had been very specific about no visitors. The press badgered us all at first and then with well-wishers—'

'But I'm not a reporter or a well-wisher,' Essie said urgently. 'I'm his fiancée.'

'I understand that, but…'

'*Please*. I'll take full responsibility.'

'Well, I really shouldn't.' The nurse was young and romantic and thought Miss Grey's uncle was the most fascinating and mysterious man since Heathcliff. And the way he had remained so devotedly at her bedside and was obviously being torn apart...

She glanced again at Essie. And here was his beautiful fiancée who had flown across the world to be at his side. It was all so *heart-rending*.

'All right.' Her voice was conspiratorial. 'But if there's any trouble I asked you to wait here and you ignored me. Okay?'

'There won't be any trouble.' Essie sounded much more confident than she felt and, after a nod and a smile, she followed the nurse out of the waiting area and along the corridor to a room right at the end of the white antiseptic passage.

'Miss Grey is in room 274.'

It was the last door on the left and the nurse stopped just before she reached it, indicating the pale green painted door with its square of glass two-thirds up with a nod of her blonde head.

'Thank you. Thank you so much.'

Essie waited until the nurse had turned and was walking away before she glanced through the glass into the room. The bed was positioned so it was in full view and the host of tubes and wires coming out of its occupant was daunting, but it was the bowed figure to one side of the bed that took most of Essie's attention.

Xavier was leaning forward so his elbows were resting on his knees and his head was in his hands. It was a pose of utter dejection.

Essie's hand went to her throat and she gripped her flesh as she prayed, silently and vehemently, for the right words to say. She had let him down once; he had peeled away the layers of self-protection and invulnerability he had built around himself and left himself wide open and she hadn't recognised the quality of the gift he was giving her. It had been all of him, every little bit of him, the complete and total whole.

She had to make him understand now; somehow, he had to believe that she loved him and it was nothing to do with guilt or pity or anything else—not even the knowledge of how much she had failed him.

She made a small inarticulate sound in her throat and it was at that moment—as though the echo of her anguish and remorse had touched something inside him—that he turned and glanced at the door.

Xavier had been sitting by Candy's bed for what seemed like an endless eternity as he watched for some sign—however faint—that she was coming back to the real world. He had been talking to her constantly, willing her to fight, to live, endeavouring to give her every bit of his strength and his determination.

But he was tired. He knew he was tired without the damn doctors and nurses nagging him to rest. He had told them he'd take all the rest he needed once he knew she was going to pull through, but until then...

He still couldn't believe it was real. Even now, after days and nights in this sterile white box, he couldn't believe it. She had been so vibrant, so beautiful, so alive, and now she was a pale, slender ghost whose breathing barely disturbed the white cotton sheets. Oh, Natalie, *Natalie*, I'm sorry. I should have protected her better, spent less time out of the country—*something*.

And the image of another sylph-like young woman—this time with deep violet-blue eyes and hair the colour of ripe corn—had been in the room, too. Even in the midst of his anguish and pain over Candy, Essie had been tearing at him.

He had never believed in crying over spilt milk and he would be the first to say that you couldn't lose what you had never had, but that was before he had met Essie. Essie—such a ridiculous name for such a beautiful woman…

His head was in his hands and he pressed his palms to either side of his temple as though he could squeeze out the images that were packed in his mind. He had to get the victory over this, and he had to do it before he went mad. If Candy came round—no, *when* Candy came round, she was going to need him more than she had ever done and he would have to be strong for her. But knowing that still couldn't stop him from seeing Essie in every slim, golden-haired woman, from hearing her voice at the oddest moments, from smelling the scent of her perfume when no one else was in the room…

Dammit, how he wanted her, *needed* her, right at this moment; he would give ten years of his life—who was he kidding? He'd give twenty, thirty years—to go back to before the time he'd told her how he felt and killed any chance they might have had for the future.

But he couldn't go back—he had to go forward, although how he was going to do that he didn't know at the moment. The future stretched before him like a bottomless black hole and, for the first time in his adult life, he felt scared. Scared that he couldn't be what Candy needed, scared that he was losing the handle on his work, his life, but most of all scared at the prospect of walking down the weeks and months and years without ever seeing Essie's face again.

Xavier's jaw tightened. What the hell? He'd always despised whingers and he was damned if anyone—man or woman—was going to turn him into one. He'd get through this the way he'd got through everything else and, if Candy was spared, he would never ask for anything else for the rest of his life. He loved Essie— he would always love her—but she belonged to a brief, sweet step out of time that had no basis in reality. He had to get that through his head.

She was thousands of miles away across the other side of the world, but it could be light years across the universe for all the difference it made.

And then he glanced up, looking towards the door, without knowing why.

He stared at the face looking through the glass and then screwed up his eyes as he raked the hair back from his forehead. His heart had given a mighty kick against his ribs and he felt sick at what he'd imagined. The nurses were constantly checking on Candy—there was forever someone or other peering in at them—but this time it had been Essie's face he'd seen and it scared him to death. He really *was* losing his mind, he thought caustically. Wouldn't some of his more predatory business competitors just love that!

And then he opened his eyes again as the door creaked, and she was standing no more than five or six feet away, her incredible blue eyes fixed on his and her lovely face as white as a sheet.

'Xavier?' Essie's voice was little more than a whisper, but she suddenly found that she had no strength left. He was looking at her so strangely, not moving, not even seeming to breathe. 'I had to come. When I heard, I had to come.'

'Essie?'

Her voice brought him out of the trance, and then, as a nurse entered the room behind Essie, saying briskly, 'We need to make Candy a little more comfortable, Mr Grey, so if you wouldn't mind leaving for a few minutes?' he nodded abruptly, his eyes never leaving Essie's strained face.

'We'll be in the coffee lounge.'

'All right, Mr Grey, there's no hurry. We'll be a little while.'

He looked so tired. So big and dark and handsome, but tired, *exhausted*, Essie thought weakly as Xavier took her elbow and walked with her into the corridor beyond the room.

'What are you doing here, Essie?' He looked down at her briefly as he led her along—a dark, unrevealing glance, but she had seen that stunned look in his eyes earlier—she had *seen* it—and it gave her the courage to answer him.

'I wanted to be near you.' Only the truth would do now. 'I *had* to be near you. I love you so much and the last two weeks have been so awful—'

'Don't put us both through this, Essie.' The words were wrenched out of him. 'It's not that I don't appreciate you coming—although it was crazy—but you were very sure of how you felt two weeks ago. And nothing's changed—'

'You're right, nothing has changed,' she said urgently. 'I loved you then and I knew it but I was too terrified to admit it, too bound up in the past. Perhaps your leaving was what it needed to make me see—I don't know—but suddenly I realised I...I couldn't live without you.'

She gulped hard, her eyes shining with tears, and as he glanced down at her again he made a sound deep in his throat, running a hand through his hair in a gesture of violent distraction.

He hadn't shaved for some time—there was at least a couple of days' growth of beard—and it made him look even tougher, sexier, but he hadn't been tough with her, Essie thought as a pang of something hot and painful sliced through her.

She couldn't lose him. She had to make him understand. Her throat was tight with fear that it might be too late as she said, 'Please believe me, Xavier, because I don't know what to say or do to convince you. I was stupid and weak and cowardly, and I know I don't deserve another chance—'

'*Don't say that.*' His hand was still on her elbow and it tightened involuntarily before he took hold of himself, drawing in a deep, steadying breath as he forced his voice into a calmer mode. 'You deserve every good thing you get out of life, Essie, and I wish you every good thing. Does that make you feel better? But my mother married her first husband out of gratitude or some such emotion, when he provided a way of escape from the miserable home life she'd endured, and it was a disaster.'

'Xavier, *listen* to me!' Her voice was too loud in the hushed clinical surroundings and this time his glance was startled. They had just reached the small coffee lounge—the counter at the far end that sold sandwiches and snacks had long since closed for the night, but the vending machines were still on duty—and Essie was eternally grateful it was deserted as she pushed open the glass doors and pulled Xavier through.

'I came here to tell you I love you.' She was holding fast to his jacket now, her hands gripping his arms just above his elbows as she stared up into his beloved face. 'I don't *care* about the practice or the house or you buying it for me. Can't you get that through your head? I went to your offices to tell you that today. It was a wonderful gift but it doesn't matter, not a jot, and if that makes me the most ungrateful person in the world, so be it.'

'Essie—'

'No, you let me finish. Don't you *dare* say anything,' she said fiercely, fighting back the tears with all her might as she struggled to make him understand. She was aware her lower lip was trembling like a child's and his eyes were stricken, but she had to say it all.

'I can't exist without you. I can't be in the same world as you are and know you are breathing and living and having a separate life to me, that you might go a whole day or a week or a year and not think of me at all. I can't bear it! I—I want to mean everything to you. I want to be your wife and have your ba—your babies...'

The last was a wail and it was too much for Xavier. He pulled her into him with a savage movement that spoke of his hunger, covering her face with kisses as he murmured incoherent words of love against her wet, salty skin.

They clung together, hearts racing and mouths fusing as they rocked in an agony of need, Essie's whole being singing with the knowledge that it was going to be all right. He believed her—she had seen it in his face, the second before he had kissed her.

It was some moments before he put her from him slightly, in order to look into her radiant upturned face, and then his voice was husky when he said, 'I love you, my bright, shining star.'

'And I love you.' She smiled at him through her tears. 'I've been so stupid, Xavier, and all this with Candy—I wasn't there for you when you needed me most.'

'No more of that.' He stroked his hand along her cheek, the silver-blue eyes that could be so cold inexpressibly tender. 'Candy will get well. Anything is possible when we are together.'

'And you forgive me?'

'There is nothing to forgive.' He pulled her close again, holding her against his heart. 'You were wary, frightened, and after your experience of the opposite sex—your stepfather who should have protected you and cared for you, and Andrew who used your vulnerability to manipulate and control—who could blame you for being unnerved by this big, brash Canadian who swept in, all guns firing?'

He smiled at her as she moved back enough in his embrace to wrap her arms round his neck. 'Big, but never brash.' Her heart was in her eyes as she looked at him and it told Xavier all he ever wanted to know.

She was his—utterly and for ever, as he was hers.

EPILOGUE

ESSIE and Xavier were married on a white-gold beach in the Caribbean four months later. The setting signified to both of them the putting away of the past and all its hurts and disappointments and, as they stood on the clean, sea-washed, virgin sand, just as the sun began to sink in a blaze of indigo and gold and scarlet, Essie's heart was soaring as high as the endless heavens.

She wore a long, ethereal, short-sleeved silk chiffon dress in pale gold, her hair threaded with tiny white orchids which were reflected in the small posy in her hands, and her feet were bare.

The velvet feel of the hot, powdery sand, the dancing waves lit with the rosy rays of the dying sun, and Xavier—tall and dark and devastatingly handsome at the side of her—was almost more than she could bear.

She didn't deserve such happiness, she told herself mistily, glancing across at Candy who, as though she had been waiting for her eyes, smiled encouragingly from her wheelchair.

They had been promised that Candy would fully recover in time, but for now the slender, red-haired beauty looked delicate and fragile in her bridesmaid's dress of white silk threaded with tiny gold flowers across the bodice.

They had delayed the wedding in order that Candy would be well enough to be Essie's attendant—something both girls had set their hearts on—and the doctors had been united in agreeing that the thought of the proposed nuptials had roused Candy out of the terrible apathy she had fallen into when she had first regained consciousness.

But for now Essie wasn't thinking of Candy—much as she had grown to love Xavier's niece, or any other of their respective friends and relations whom Xavier had flown out for the wedding. Her heart and soul and mind were fixed on Xavier.

He was holding her hand tightly as the minister led them through their vows, his big, lean body clothed in a loose white silk shirt that had no collar and was unbuttoned at the neck, and white linen trousers.

The paleness of his clothes emphasised his dark, virile masculinity a hundredfold, and he made Essie's legs weak. He looked sexy and warm and breathtakingly handsome, and he was hers. *He was hers.*

She glanced at her engagement ring on her right hand, where she had moved it temporarily for the ceremony, and the exquisite star of diamonds looked back at her.

'You're my Esther, my star,' Xavier had whispered as he had slid it onto her finger a few days after she had flown to him in Canada, four months before. 'My bright morning star, my sun, my moon, my universe. My reason for living.'

And she was. She knew she was. And now the moment was here.

'I do.' Her voice was loud and clear and confident as she spoke the words that would unite them as man and wife, and her smile was sweet as Xavier glanced down at her, his love for her turning his eyes into liquid silver pools.

They had found each other. Against all the odds they had found each other, and she would never let him go. He was her everything and she was his, and the future was theirs to share.

Two hearts beating as one and a love that was endless.

'And I now pronounce you man and wife. Xavier, you may kiss the bride.'

And he did!